THE CELLAR'S SECRET

First Publication December 2024
Indies United Publishing House, LLC

ISBN: 978-1-64456-777-7 [paperback]
ISBN: 978-1-64456-778-4 [Kindle]
ISBN: 978-1-64456-779-1 [ePub]

Library of Congress Control Number: 2024920502

INDIES UNITED PUBLISHING HOUSE, LLC
P.O. BOX 3071
QUINCY, IL 62305-3071
indiesunited.net

THE KIKI MOORE SERIES

THE CELLAR'S SECRET

B. PAYTON SETTLES

INDIES UNITED PUBLISHING HOUSE, LLC

CHAPTER ONE

R-R-Ring!

The sound of the clunky black phone on the teacher's desk broke through Kiki Moore's daydream. She looked up from her mostly blank essay paper and traded glances with Norma, the other eighth-grader at their tiny country school.

Miss Jepson, standing next to the desk with her lethal pointing stick, reached for the phone. "It's not supposed to ring while school is in session. Someone doesn't know the rules."

"You think it's about you?" Norma, a placid, freckle-faced redhead, leaned into the aisle and whispered to Kiki.

Kiki's family had been at this location—Napa, California, a short drive from Hamilton Air Force Base in nearby Novato—longer than anywhere else since the war started. The two Moore girls made friends, caught up on their school work, and felt at home. Kiki knew they wouldn't be here forever--they were, after all, an Air Force family--but she prayed every night for a few more months in the warm-hearted cocoon that was Napa, California.

"I hope not," Kiki stretched her thin frame and pulled absentmindedly on one of her dark brown braids. A month ago, when the grisly history of her family's ranch was revealed—Kiki found a body hidden in the attic of an abandoned house—the calls had all been about her. Gradually the school's farming community had turned its attention to other things—World War II, the awful-tasting, rust-colored water in local wells, and the yearly Grange Hall square dance. The phone had stopped it's incessant ringing.

Miss Jepson's quiet, "Browns Valley School, Miss Jepson speaking … Really, Mrs. Moore? All right, if it's absolutely necessary," floated across eighteen bowed heads to the back of the room.

Gulp. Kiki put her pencil down.

Twenty minutes later she sat on the schoolhouse steps, waiting for her family's Ford sedan to appear. The school yard was quiet, disturbed only by the hum of a bee and the occasional screech of a blue jay. The setting had a calming effect; Kiki breathed in the warm, eucalyptus-scented playground air and became conscious of energy still present after the morning recess: Traces of giggling on the swings, a muffled shout at the tetherball pole. She gave herself a shake, trying to shut down her sixth sense. *I don't need that right now. It just gets me in trouble.*

Without warning a sense of profound loss engulfed her. *What's going on? Has something happened to Daddy, far away in Germany? Is that why Mama's picking me up early today?*

The Moore family's black sedan pulled into the school yard. When Kiki saw her older sister behind the wheel, her stomach clenched. *Mama took Joan out of school, too? She's letting her drive? Please God, don't let Daddy be hurt--or worse.* At sixteen, Joan had her permit and was eager to drive every chance she got. Mrs. Moore, though, had little confidence in the eager but unpracticed teen-ager.

Kiki stood, hopping from foot to foot as the sedan rolled slowly across the asphalt. The car jerked to a stop. She jumped on the running board, pulled the passenger door open and climbed in next to her mother. "Is Daddy okay?"

"No talking. I have to concentrate!" Joan stared straight ahead.

"I'll take that as a yes." Kiki looked at her mother. "I didn't get to finish my essay."

Mama nodded, but said nothing. Her profile, the sharp, straight nose and alabaster skin surrounded by jet-black hair set in a Victory roll, comforted Kiki. *She wouldn't be so calm if it was bad news.*

Kiki turned and stared out the window. *I wonder where we're going?* They'd already passed Leslie's house, on the right as you left the prune orchards and headed toward town.

When they reached the highway going south Mama said quietly, "Take the first Vallejo exit, Joan. It's less than fifteen miles after that." She turned to face Kiki. "I got you girls an appointment with Miss Coralee, the woman who gives Toni home permanents. She only had today open for the entire month, so I had to take it because," her face glowed with excitement, "we're leaving next week for New York. We're joining your father in Germany."

Kiki's mouth dropped open. She knew Mama missed Daddy; they'd been married since Mama was sixteen and Daddy was the family's absolute ruler. Hadn't he said, though, that they should stay behind, wait on the ranch for his return? Yes. He'd said Germany was in bad shape, not safe for Air Force dependents.

Kiki looked past Mama to Joan. Her sister's hands held the steering wheel in a death grip. *She's either nervous about driving, or she doesn't want to go to Germany, either.*

"Do we have to go, Mama? Everyone in Napa's been so nice to us since I found that girl's body. And, what about our 4-H projects? Joan and I can't just walk away from Grunty and the chickens."

The car surged forward; Joan must have accidentally punched the accelerator. She took her eyes off the road for a second to glance at Kiki. "Grunty? Is that old pig all you're worried about?"

"Joan! Watch the road!" Mama's tone was sharp. "Not another word out of either of you. That's an order."

Kiki huddled against the door, trying to stay quiet. She couldn't. Her mouth opened and words tumbled out. "When we moved to Napa, Daddy said we were here for good. We made friends; I like school." She felt Mama stiffen, but the words kept coming. "I want to stay here. We don't even speak German!" She cowered against the passenger door, waiting to be slapped. *What's come over me? I've never, ever sassed Mama before.*

Joan, in a voice that sounded like it came from a six-year-old, squeaked, "Is that the turn-off? Thanks for arranging the perms, Mama. I can't wait to have curly hair."

"Yes." Mama's tone was flat. "That's the turn-off. When you get to that stoplight, turn left. Her house should be at the end of the block."

Two hours later, sitting on the front porch at Miss Coralee's two-story, downtown Vallejo house and fluff-drying their now-curly hair, Kiki whispered, "Joan, how can we change Mama's mind? We can't go to Germany; we just can't!"

Joan groaned. "We have to, Kiki. It's our patriotic duty to follow Daddy. You know that. Look how many places we've lived since the war broke out." Joan held up a hand and touched each finger. "Shreveport, Louisiana, then Palmdale, South San

Francisco, Novato, Napa." She smiled. "Remember when we arrived in California in the middle of the night, that woman with canaries flying around in her spare room? It was her patriotic duty to put us on cots in there."

Kiki grinned. "I'm still sneezing from the feathers. And, don't forget the bird poop. It was everywhere."

"Yeah." Joan's smile faded. "Besides, Mama's having a hard time running the ranch on her own." She frowned. "I heard her on the phone yesterday, talking to Mrs. Borrette. She said it's too hard, managing two girls and the ranch, too."

Kiki started to speak. Joan stopped her with one of Mama's glares.

"It's true. Don't deny it. You're always getting in trouble; it was easier for Mama when Daddy was here—he understands you."

Was it true? Was this awful move her fault? Kiki leaned away from Joan and squeezed her eyes shut, oblivious to the cars rumbling by on the street, the chatter drifting through the open front door. (Miss Coralee, a weathered-looking platinum blonde, popped her gum and talked nonstop).

I wish Daddy would've told Mama about the sixth sense I got from him. Maybe then she'd understand me better. The thought startled Kiki. She straightened and glanced at Joan. *She doesn't know, either. Should I tell her? No. Daddy swore me to secrecy.*

Joan, waving at two teen-aged boys riding by in the back of a pick-up, raised an eyebrow. "What? I'm just being friendly. Lord knows there's probably no cute boys in Germany."

"You girls are going to be world travelers! Isn't that wonderful?" Miss Coralee, still talking, ushered Mama out onto the porch. "Be sure and send me a postcard."

"We're not going as tourists, Coralee." Mama laughed. "Even postcards have to go through my husband's APO address." She looked at Kiki and her smile disappeared.

Coralee ran her fingers through the young girl's still damp, kinky curls. "That's right. You're part of the Occupation. Strange world we live in, isn't it, when youngsters can walk around where Hitler and his Nazis marched?" She pulled Kiki to her aproned bosom for a half-hug. "You be careful over there, sweetie pie." When she let go, her smile was gone.

"Strange world, indeed." Mama's mouth made a straight line. "But we're used to it." She started down the steps and looked back at her daughters. "Don't dawdle. From here we go to the Base for shots. When you go to a foreign country, you need lots of inoculations."

As Kiki got into the car she took a mental snapshot of Miss Coralee's comfortable-looking grey-shingled house, settled as it was next to the sidewalk. With its' wraparound porch and washed-out exterior, it looked durable, dependable. *I wonder what German houses look like? Thatched roofs? Ivy, like the pictures on my playing card collection? They've probably all been bombed.*

From the porch railing Miss Coralee made a mock salute.

The road from Vallejo to the North Bay Area ran along a levee at the foot of San Pablo Bay. Narrow and with nothing to separate the two directions of traffic, it required all of Joan's concentration and Mama's, too. When Kiki pointed out the monstrous grey warships in the nearby Mare Island Naval Shipyard, Mama murmured, "Quiet, Kiki. Joan mustn't take her eyes off the road."

Kiki turned away, staring out the window at salt flats stretching for miles to the hazy, distant mountains. Her thoughts turned to Miss Coralee's final words. *Why'd she say that, about us being careful? Does she know what happened to me on the ranch? Mama wouldn't tell her, would she?*

Joan's even, quiet voice broke through Kiki's thoughts. "My friend's mom works at the shipyards. She makes warships —maybe not now the war's over. That's so keen, though. Like

Rosie the Riveter. You could have done that, Mama."

"Eyes forward, Joan. No talking." Mama stared straight ahead.

When they pulled in through Hamilton Air Force Base's whitewashed stucco gates, the guard on duty looked in their car and grinned. Joan, smiling back at him, fluffed her curls. As they moved along the road beyond the gate, she said, "Thanks for the perms, Mama. I love mine."

Kiki groaned. "My scalp hurts. Those chemicals burned."

That night, when Joan came into the shadowy bedroom and slipped onto the bottom bunk she whispered, "Kiki?"

Kiki peered over the edge of the top bunk. "What?"

"You have to stop pouting. For Mama."

Kiki sat up, leaning on her elbow. Her frizzy hair brushed the ceiling. "What do you mean, pouting? Did Mama say something to you? I'm not pouting." She lay back down and pulled the covers over her head.

After a minute Joan whispered, "You think Mama really wants to go where there's *Nazis*?"

Kiki cringed at the hated word. *Yes, Mama wants to go. She wants to be with Daddy.*

Joan sighed. "As Daddy's kids, it's our job to help Mama. You know that. Even if it means leaving our friends." Joan's face brightened. "When we get back here, we'll be celebrities. No one else in this Podunk town goes anywhere, let alone to Germany!"

Kiki couldn't help smiling; Joan's mood was contagious. She put her head back on the pillow. "Go to bed, Silly. Or should I say, Sergeant Joan?" Then, "I'll try to be cheerful for Mama. Sweet dreams."

The next few days were a blur of activity, with Mama barking orders like a drill sergeant. Between getting the ranch ready for tenants and packing to live in a foreign country, she was frantic. When Debarkation Day, as Joan called it, came, Kiki was almost glad. At least now Mama would calm down and maybe get some sleep. A cross-country train ride, a visit to New York City, an ocean voyage? Anticipation of all that drove fear to the back of Kiki's mind.

The Oakland train station platform swarmed with military uniforms of all kinds. Mama took one look at the crowd and plunged in, pulling her sleepy daughters along in the pre-dawn adventure. The girls hurried to keep up; the crowd's excitement made Kiki dizzy.

"Can you believe it? It's really happening. We're going overseas!" Joan sounded a little scared.

Kiki, grinning, hopped onto the steps of the Pullman car behind Mama. "And taking a train across the whole country!"

The girls quickly adjusted to life on a moving train. Their seats in the Pullman car converted to bunk beds at night, with curtains to shield them from anyone walking by in the aisle. In the daytime the Club car, with its food and friendly people, was just a few swaying steps away.

On the second night—it was after midnight, and inside the Pullman all was quiet—Kiki woke and pushed back the window shade. What she saw took her breath away. A full moon shone on a sparkling white landscape that stretched endlessly in every direction. Absolutely flat, not a tree or bush visible, it looked sunken—like a gigantic, empty bowl. "Where are we," she muttered. "Are we still on planet earth?'

From the berth below came Mama's whispered, "It's the Great Salt Lake, Kiki. We're crossing Utah. Isn't it beautiful?"

It took three more days to reach New York City, where they were to board the ship to Europe. After the cozy, encapsulating atmosphere of the train, the cavernous, confusing Grand Central Station was frightening. When Kiki saw her own fear reflected in Mama's face, she realized how vulnerable they were, alone and so far from home. She grabbed Joan's arm and held on tight.

Mama managed to find the army bus taking them from the station to a barracks at Fort Hamilton, their next stop in this journey. The drive through downtown New York City (movie newsreels had pictured it as full of ecstatic people celebrating the victory over Hitler) was cold and uncomfortable. The bus, designed for transporting soldiers, featured unpadded metal seats close together.

When Kiki rubbed a clear spot on the window and peered out—the glass fogged up immediately on this November day— she saw only sour-faced, shivering men carrying protest signs through piles of dirty snow.

"Union strikers," Mama whispered in response to Kiki's raised eyebrows.

The strikers' intensity and the bleakness of their task as they trudged the sidewalk in the freezing weather frightened Kiki. She tilted her head and looked up, up, along concrete skyscraper walls. *New York is so alien --will Germany be worse?* The benign, slow-paced world of Napa was very far away.

For the next few days Ft. Hamilton, with its old, two-story brick barracks and guarded gates, soothed Kiki. When Mama announced that the troopship Jarret S. Huddleston was in port and it was time to pack their bags, the girl's anxiety returned. *Are we really doing this? Going to the land of swastikas and concentration camps?*

Without thinking she wandered outside, saw a bus at the curb and climbed in. Two hours later, looking out the window as the bus made another trip around the base, she saw Mama and Joan on the sidewalk. *Uh, oh. I've done it again.* Kiki sighed; the family's first rule—be a help to your mother—asserted itself. She walked the length of the bus to the front, waited while the driver opened the hydraulic door, and stepped off.

It wasn't until an hour later on the gangplank leading to the deck of the U.S.S. Jarret S. Huddleston that Mama hissed. "Your father will hear about this."

Kiki gulped. Daddy probably still had his leather belt.

CHAPTER TWO

Mama and Joan kept a close watch on Kiki in the hours until the ship raised anchor and left Brooklyn's Port of New York. They needn't have. Standing on deck as the grey metal troopship ploughed through Upper New York Bay to the open ocean, sea breeze in her frizzy hair and salt tickling her nostrils, Kiki felt awed and grateful. When she spotted the Statue of Liberty with its raised torch, her fears faded. *That statue stands for strength and courage. I'll take a helping of that.*

Some of the families they'd met on the train and at Ft. Hamilton were passengers on the Jarret S. Huddleston, too. After finding their stateroom (down steep metal stairs and along a corridor to a gunmetal grey closet barely large enough for bunk beds and a single berth) the Moores connected with friends in this new, floating 'neighborhood.'

"Mama," Kiki gazed longingly as Joan and two other teens drifted away, talking in whispers. "You don't have to worry about me. I'm sorry I got on that bus. I won't do anything like that here." She hoped her expression was pathetic enough to get Mama to let go of her hand.

Mama, busy chatting with another woman, ignored Kiki at first. After a minute she muttered. "I wish I could believe that." She tightened her grip.

Kiki stared at the floor. *Mama hates me. She'll probably lock me in the stateroom forever.*

In the dining room that evening—the passengers and ship's officers ate together at cloth-covered tables with china and silverware—Kiki sat miserably beside her mother, mortified at being treated like a naughty four-year-old in this impressively adult setting. When the captain smiled at her, her father's energy washed over her. She glanced at Mama. *She's not frowning anymore. She feels Daddy's presence, too.*

A bowl of soup was set in front of Kiki; she fingered the silverware doubtfully. *Which spoon do I use? There are so many.*

Joan, giggling, stage-whispered, "Use the soup spoon, dummy!"

Mama glared at Joan, then guided Kiki's hand to the roundest spoon in the set. "That one. The one on the outside. See?" Her tone was gentle.

Is she over being mad? Kiki tried to catch Mama's eye; Mama looked away. *Maybe.*

The next morning—all three of the Moores slept soundly in their gently rocking bunks—Kiki got a talking-to while Mama wet-brushed the girl's wiry tangles.

"I want you to promise you'll talk to me first if you get any strange compulsions. We must not have a repeat of the bus ride disaster." Nose to nose, Mama looked in her daughter's eyes.

"Yes, ma'am. I will." Kiki crossed her heart and looked fearfully back, then let herself be hugged as Mama whispered, "Let's start over and try to enjoy being sailors."

Life aboard a ship crossing the Atlantic was unlike anything Kiki could have imagined. The communal nature of the experience—the passengers ate in the officers' mess, participated in organized activities and had free range of the main deck, weather permitting—brought with it a comforting sense of extended family. The children on board, bonded anyway as military dependents, moved about in groups and were soon labeled the 'Ship Rats.'

On the third day out, Joan asked Mama if she could be in charge of Kiki. "She'll be okay, Mama. She loves the ship. She's not scared anymore. Please? That way, you can relax a little. You can play bridge with the other moms."

Mama, standing next to the bunks in her blue wool dress with the matching sweater, looked thoughtfully down at Kiki. "Promise there will be no more monkey business?"

Kiki nodded. "Yes ma'am. Cross my heart and hope to die." As she said the last part, she gulped. *Hope **not** to die, I mean.*

It was November; the crossing was stormy and cold. Most days it wasn't safe to be on deck—being swept overboard into the black, choppy water was a real possibility—and when the dinner plates slid back and forth across the dining table, Kiki was very glad for tabletops with borders.

They sailed into the worst storm—wind and rain fierce enough to turn the Atlantic into mountains and valleys of water

—after midnight the tenth day out. Kiki, jerked out of a dream of howling monsters, was tossed off the bottom bunk onto the floor. As she landed, she saw Joan's pajamaed legs hanging over the edge of the top bunk.

"Don't land on me!" Kiki's scream was lost in the howling wind. At that moment the ship seemed to stand on end, then plunge down like a roller coaster. The stateroom door swung open and everything under the bunks—suitcases, boxes, shoes —slid out to the passageway, then back.

"Hang on!" Mama's shout was followed by a loud **CRACK** as the ship shuddered, righted itself, then tipped the other way.

Joan dropped down onto Kiki's bunk and wrapped her arms around the metal frame. "Take the other end," she shouted.

Kiki scrambled off the floor and grasped the bedframe's cold metal tubing. She whispered, "Our Father who art in heaven, we could use some help down here."

When, hours later, the storm was behind them and sunlight came weakly through the port hole, Kiki felt Mama's hand on her shoulder. "Wake up, sleepy head. We have a mess to clean up."

Weather kept them below deck for most of the trip. The last evening before arrival at the Port of London, though, the sky was clear—cold, but free of wind or clouds. The older kids gathered on the ship's bow, lounging against metal storage chests and talking quietly. The next day they'd be scattered to base camps set up all over Germany; most would never meet again. There was a touch of sadness in their excited whispers.

Joan, with uncharacteristic kindness, brought Kiki along to the teen meeting. Kiki was grateful to be included; she sat quietly next to her sister in the campfire-style circle, studying everyone for cues on how to act. *At least there's no silverware to decipher.*

One of the boys, a gangly, greasy-haired youth named Ethan whose hands and feet were way too big for the rest of him, smiled at her. "So. Kiki, is it?" His voice, soft, confidential, only cracked once. "Joan's little sister?"

Before Kiki could respond he continued, "Back home in Napa, you found a dead body and gave some old codger a heart attack? Impressive. Tell us about it."

Kiki felt a blush rising up her cheeks. *How does he know?* She stared at Joan. *Is that why you brought me here? To be entertainment for this pimple-faced goon?*

Joan lifted her chin and smirked, but said nothing.

"C'mon, kid. Don't be shy. We're your friends. It's our last night aboard this floating bathtub. Who we gonna tell?"

The other teens--three boys and two girls--looked from Ethan to Kiki, as if waiting for the show to start.

Kiki felt sick to her stomach. She bent over, clenching her fists against the ever-present throbbing of the ship's engine and the slap, slap of water against the hull. From elsewhere on the ship, she heard the strains of music: Glen Miller's, *"I've got a girl, in Kalamazoo ..."*

"I get it. This shy stuff is part of the act." Ethan's laugh sounded high, like a hyena. "You'll love Germany. Those Krauts got a lotta secrets." He grinned. "You're from California, right? You meet the old codger on one of those beaches?"

Kiki got to her feet, blinking back tears. Without looking at anyone she stepped out of the circle and headed across the deck to the nearest hatch.

"Don't leave, Kiki." The tall, sweet-faced blonde sitting next to Hyena-Laugh—her name was Kathleen and she was his sister—jumped up. "Stop torturing her, Ethan. What did she ever do to you?" She turned and followed Kiki through the hatch.

"Wait up, Kiki," Kathleen called. "Don't pay any attention to Ethan. He's just getting back at Joan because she wouldn't let him kiss her."

Kiki stopped, but didn't turn around until she felt the older girl's hand on her shoulder.

"But," Kiki whispered, "he knows ... stuff ... about me. She told him. Why would she do that? It was awful, what happened. I still have nightmares."

Kathleen hooked an arm through Kiki's. "I'll walk you back to your stateroom. Is your mom there? She needs to hear about this."

"What did Joan say?" Kiki allowed herself to be guided along the passageway. "I didn't kill anybody, honest. That man kidnapped me. He had a heart attack after the sheriff caught him. It was awful." She gulped. "Why would Joan gossip about me?"

"To impress my brother, maybe? Ethan's disgustingly popular with girls." Kathleen shrugged, as if it was beyond her comprehension.

Kiki shook her head. "She sacrificed me for a boy? That's just mean! I never want to be a teen-ager."

They'd reached the Moores' stateroom. Mrs. Moore's laughter could be heard through the partly open door.

Fear rippled through Kiki "She's got company. Let's not go in yet." Would Mama understand? Would she think Kiki was acting up again? *I don't want to find out.*

"We have to. My brother's not going to get away with what he did." Kathleen stepped to the stateroom door and rapped her knuckles on it. "Mrs. Moore? It's Kathleen Wilson and Kiki."

Mama looked out, saw the two girls and frowned. "What happened? Where's Joan? Is she okay?" She looked away, into the stateroom. "Do you mind, Vera? Looks like there's a problem here."

Vera? Oh, no! Her husband is daddy's commanding officer. Mama will be so mad at me. Kiki groaned.

"Joan's fine, Mrs. Moore." Kathleen spoke fast. "One of the boys was rude and hurt Kiki's feelings. I thought you should know *someone* spread a mean lie about her."

The woman named Vera peered around Mama's shoulder, glanced at the girls, and said, "We'll talk later, Emily." Then, with a quick smile to Mama, she slipped out of the stateroom and disappeared along the passageway.

Mrs. Moore backed away from the door and perched on one of the bunks. "Thank you, Kathleen. Go on back to the group; I'll take it from here." She didn't attempt a smile as the older girl gave Kiki a quick hug and disappeared along the passageway.

"Don't be mad, Mama. Please. I shouldn't have gone with Joan. Those kids are too old for me." Kiki sat next to her mother, staring at her hands. *Please God, don't let me be in trouble again.*

"What was this 'mean lie' Kathleen mentioned? The only person in that group who knows anything about you is Joan." Mama's face was stern, but her eyes were soft.

Maybe she's not mad.

Kiki told her what the boy—Ethan—had said. "Kathleen said he was getting back at Joan for not letting him kiss her." Kiki mimicked Kathleen's gagging gesture.

Mama put an arm around Kiki and hugged her. "If we see Kathleen tomorrow, let's be sure to thank her for rescuing you." She paused. "I'll talk to Joan. Gossiping about you to impress her friends? Reprehensible." She smiled gently. "Look it up, dear."

When Joan stepped through the doorway an hour later, Mama took her by the arm and whisked her out of the stateroom. "Stay there, Kiki, and finish your packing. We'll be back in a minute."

Joan looks scared. Good.

The U.S.S. Barret S. Huddleston docked at Wapping Harbor

in the Port of London the next day.

The process of getting passengers to shore—it seemed to Kiki that she, Mama and Joan went from one long line to the next for hours—took the entire day. When they finally stood on firm land—a wooden dock, actually, but not moving at all—Kiki smiled until she thought her face would crack. Joan, hanging onto Mama's arm, smiled, too until she looked at Kiki. Then she frowned and looked away.

Does she feel bad about last night? No. She's mad at me because she got in trouble.

Kiki turned away, shivering, and looked down at her feet. Her shoes—thin leather cut below the ankle—were soaked from the melting slush. She couldn't feel her toes at all. *Why did I get off that bus back there in New York? It's freezing here and my sister hates me.*

In the light of early evening, the port's devastation from bombings was nightmarish. Parts of walls with roofs caved in, door frames with no walls around them, gates standing open to steps going nowhere. Kiki's suitcase bumped against a wooden crate and a rat ran across her foot. "Eeek!" She jumped away.

"Crossed the Atlantic in November for this, did you, miss? A fool's errand, I'd say." A dirty, haggard-looking old man sitting with his back against a pile of rubble winked up at Kiki.

Mama, standing nearby, slipped an arm around her younger daughter. "Stand here by Joan and me. We'll stay warm together." The smile she gave the old man was tight-lipped.

"Look, Mama, those jeeps! I bet that's our ride to the train station." Joan stepped off the dock onto the cobbled road.

The rest of that day was a blur. The ride to Frankfurt, in what was little more than a cattle car, made their earlier train trip across the United States seem elegant: The nine hours were spent on narrow metal seats with no heat, no food, and a cold metal toilet in a closet.

Kiki had the window seat, with Joan squeezed in next to her and Mama on the aisle. As she stared out into the dark, the ranch back home seemed like little more than a fairy tale. She rested her forehead against the glass. *Will Daddy be glad to see us?*

"Mama?" Joan's whisper startled Kiki. "If Germany's wrecked as bad as London, where will we live?"

"Daddy found us a house." Mama's voice was quiet.

"Did it belong to a German family? What happened to them?" Kiki's breath made fog on the window.

"The Occupied Forces--that's us--commandeers homes for their officers. That's what happens when a country loses a war." Mama's soft voice was drowned out by the train's hissing and grinding.

Kiki looked out the window. On the side of one roofless building a sign proclaimed, *Willkommen to Deutschland.*

CHAPTER THREE

As the train approached the Wiesbaden station, Kiki cleared a spot on the window and looked out at darkness and swirling snowflakes.

"Let me know when you see something." Mama touched Kiki's shoulder.

Broken brick walls and barbed wire emerged first, then a dimly lit stone platform guarded by ... an angel? *Yes. It is an angel!* As tall as a person, the angel's wings were spread and its face turned upward. Kiki's heart lurched. *It looks frozen in take-off. I know just how you feel, Herr Angel.*

Kiki saw the word **WIESBADEN** printed on the one remaining wall of a bombed building. "We're here, Mama!"

Mama and Joan crowded next to Kiki for a view of the men huddled together on the train platform. Stamping their boots and talking in bursts of steamy air, they looked cold in spite of their woolen overcoats, caps, and gloves.

"Look, Mama: the one in the back. Is that Daddy?" Kiki felt her shoulders relax for the first time in ages.

"Maybe." Mama's face lit up.

The train stopped, the exit doors opened and travelers poured out. Mama, Joan and Kiki shuffled along the aisle, pausing at the door. "Do you see him?"

"Keep moving!" A woman behind them snapped.

As Kiki turned around she heard, from somewhere on the platform. "Moore family! Over here!"

Mama, Joan and Kiki hopped down onto the snow-blotched wooden platform, Kiki sprinting toward that call. She dodged around slower-moving bodies, shouting, "Daddy! Daddy!"

"Hey!"

She spun on her heel to avoid crashing into an embracing couple, glanced toward the luggage car, and saw her father.

Colonel Moore stood leaning against the metal wall of a boxcar, looking handsome and relaxed in his long green overcoat, colonel's cap, and gloves. Kiki slowed to a self-conscious walk. He wasn't smiling. Had she done something wrong, already? No. As she got closer, she saw his dark eyes twinkling.

Joan and Mama plunged past. Daddy opened his arms and wrapped Mama in a hug, then released her and turned to his daughters. "Welcome to Germany, girls!" His voice was husky.

The two-hour drive from Wiesbaden to Bad Kissingen was a cold one. Daddy's Jeep, a sort of convertible, had a canvas top with buttoned flaps instead of windows. It had no heater, and the canvas was no protection against the frigid air. When Daddy glanced back at Joan and Kiki huddled under a wool blanket, he chuckled. "In case you didn't know it, girls, the North Pole is just a few miles from here."

"The North Pole? Where Santa lives?" Mama laughed so infectiously both girls had to giggle, too.

"Don't forget, Daddy, we're from California. We've never

lived in a freezer." Joan's teeth chattered as she spoke.

"Get used to it." The dismissal in Daddy's tone was all too familiar.

Kiki pulled the blanket up around her ears and peeked out through a side flap. When snowflakes stung her face she pulled back, blinked the flakes from her eyelashes and looked through the windshield instead.

The headlights could barely penetrate the falling snow on the tree-lined road. *We sure got out of the city fast.* Occasionally Kiki spotted a heap of brick, a broken fence, or the arch of a stone bridge. She ducked under the blanket and snuggled closer to Joan. *She's mean and sneaky but she's warm.*

"Are we almost there, Daddy?" Joan's voice was loud in the jeep's cocoon-like silence.

Daddy nodded. Mama looked back at the girls, then at her husband. "Will we be able to stay in the house tonight, Bill? Does it have water and electricity?"

"*Jah wohl,*" Daddy smiled at Mama. "I got a cord of wood for the fireplace. The girls' room has one big bed. They can keep each other warm."

"Are there Nazis in Bad Kissingen, Daddy?" Kiki looked hesitantly at Mama as she spoke. *I hope that's an okay question. I don't want to upset Daddy.*

Colonel Moore's eyes met Kiki's in the rearview mirror. "Of course, Kiki. This is Germany." He frowned. "You won't see German soldiers, though. They've either left the country or they're hunkered down trying to make it through the winter." He cranked the steering wheel to the right; the Jeep turned off the main road. "We're almost there, Emily. This is *Vierstrausse* , the street our house is on."

Kiki and Joan both sat up and looked out the flaps as the Jeep bounced along *Viersträusse's* cobblestones. With no streetlights and no light coming from houses, they saw only the outline of roofs against the night sky.

"People go to bed early in Germany." Joan sounded uneasy. "Early and hungry." Daddy glanced out his side window, frowning.

When they pulled into a graveled driveway near the end of the lane, their headlights revealed a two-story brick house with steep front steps flanked by tall bushes. The dark, sharply peaked roof reminded Kiki of a witch's hat. She gulped and crowded closer to Joan.

"This is it, Emily. Home sweet home." Col. Moore leaned across and gave his wife a quick kiss. "I hope you won't be sorry you came."

"As long as I'm with you, I'll be happy." Mama touched his cheek, then looked back at the girls. "Grab your suitcases. Stay close. Kiki, I want you right behind me."

When Daddy unlocked the front door and stepped into the dark, cold house, Kiki's impression was of dead air. In contrast to the sharp coldness outside, the house smelled stuffy, stale. She sneezed.

Daddy switched on the front hall light to a room fully furnished and with the look of occupants still in residence. A sweater hung on an ornate, mirrored coat rack; a magazine lay on one arm of a cushioned green couch.

Mama hesitated. "It feels like we're intruding. Are you sure the family's not coming back?"

Daddy stopped in the kitchen doorway. "It was a Jewish family, Emily. They aren't coming back." He started up the stairs. "Come on, girls. You're going to bed."

The upstairs hall, a square, white space lined in dark wood, had four doors, all closed. Daddy opened three of them, one after the other. "Bathroom," he leaned in and turned on the bathroom light, "kids' room," he switched on the light in a small room almost entirely taken up by a four-poster double bed, "and our room, Emily." He turned on the light in the room next to the bathroom.

"Is that the linen closet?" Mama indicated the fourth door.

"Nope. That goes to the maid's quarters, in the attic." Daddy smiled. "The *fräuleins* work cheap; you're getting a maid, Emily."

There's an attic? Someone lives up there? Kiki thought of the abandoned house in Napa. She shuddered.

Daddy glanced at her, then turned to Mama. "Get these girls to bed, Emily. I'll meet you in the kitchen in ten minutes."

Joan had been very quiet during the tour of the house. After Daddy went downstairs she chattered with Mama, ignoring Kiki. "Isn't it wonderful, being with Daddy again? You look so happy, Mama. You're glowing!"

Kiki was too tired to care about anything, even this cold, creepy house. She washed her face, dug pajamas out of her duffel bag and climbed into bed. It wasn't until Mama kissed them goodnight and left the room that Joan spoke to her.

"Kiki? I'm really sorry about what happened on the ship. I should have known Ethan would make fun of you." Joan gulped. It sounded, in the dark, quiet room, like she was crying.

Kiki stiffened. *Is she apologizing? That's a first.* Anger washed over her. "You're just saying that because you're scared. You don't care about my feelings."

Joan wiped her sleeve across her nose. "Maybe," she finally said. "Germany is scary. I do care about your feelings, though. Some. Besides, you're much stronger than me."

Kiki turned over so she was facing her sister. "I'm stronger? You're sixteen, for cripe's sake." She flipped over and pounded her pillow. "End of conversation. Go to sleep." As she closed her eyes she heard Joan murmur, "Older. Not stronger."

A vacation spa for tourists before the war, Bad Kissingen's hot springs and ornately decorated pools were now in ruins. The few undamaged buildings were commandeered for use by the Allies. When Kiki saw the marble statuary and broad steps leading to empty, cracked pools, she thought of the kings and queens in her book of fairy tales. *Their palaces were like this. I wonder if Germany's king—I think they called him a Kaiser—went swimming here.*

Unlike the spa, Bad Kissingen's village was spared by the bombs and, although many shops were closed, some stayed open. On the family's first tour of the quaint Bavarian town, Kiki spotted a picture of Hitler—or so she thought—in a store window. *There he is! Maybe he's not dead.* She glanced at the back of her father's head as they walked along the cobblestone street. *Should I ask Daddy? No. He'd just get mad.* After that, the colorful Tyrolean storefronts seemed ominous, unwelcoming.

At the town's towering stone gates Daddy pointed out a small hotel. "That's the Officers' Club."

"Where you lived before we got here?" Kiki's voice trailed off when two brightly-dressed young women emerged from the hotel's red double doors. They saw the Jeep and waved, calling, "*Guten morgen, Wilhelm!*"

Mama stiffened. She stared at Daddy, her eyes flashing. "Looks like I got here none too soon."

"Now, Emily." Daddy patted Mama's knee. "Don't let the *f räuliens* bother you. They're just trying to survive." He looked in the rearview mirror at the girls. "One of those women may be our new maid."

Joan muttered, "Not if Mama has anything to say about it."

The first week went by in an icy blur. The cold seeped into Kiki's bones, numbed her fingers and toes, turned her lips blue. She hated it.

"Tough it." Daddy smiled rakishly from within the folds of his heavy wool overcoat. "You want to feel sorry for someone? Look over there." He jerked a thumb toward two German boys across the street: Kiki saw thin jackets with too-short sleeves and baggy trousers above battered shoes. She stuffed her mittened hands under her armpits, frowning. One of the boys looked up and shouted, "*Schokolade, bitte?*" She turned away. *I'd give him a Hershey bar if I had one.*

The house on *Viersträusse* was full of troubled energy, and Kiki's sixth sense felt it. Mama and the new German maid, Ilse (she arrived on the doorstep the second day they were there, tall, blonde, and hard-faced) gave it a thorough cleaning, but despair still hung in the air. It was heaviest upstairs, so Kiki stayed downstairs as much as possible. Bedtime was a problem. She told herself, *I'm imagining things,* but she avoided looking in shadowed corners. Most nights she dropped off to sleep chanting her invincibility prayer, "God, please make these blankets a locked box nothing can get through."

On their third morning in the house Joan grumbled, "Get a grip, Kiki. There's nothing to be afraid of. Tell you what: The snow's melting. Let's take Daddy's dog and explore the back yard." She gave Kiki a mischievous smile. "Anything to get your mind off *Nazis* ... or Santa Claus ... or the bogey man."

Roland, Colonel Moore's German Shepherd, spent most of every day waiting by the front door for the colonel's return. Now, though, when he heard his name he stood and galloped across the foyer to the girls.

Kiki snapped the dog's leather leash onto his collar. "You'll keep us safe, won't you, boy?"

A few minutes later, staring at the back yard's bare trees, patchy grass, and boarded-up wooden shed, Joan sighed. "Ugh.

Boring. Let's sneak out front and go for a walk. Maybe we'll see a cute German boy."

"Are you kidding? Daddy said Roland's trained to attack civilians, remember? Our neighbors, the old German ladies we see walking by every day? Civilians." Kiki put a tentative hand on the dog's head. He turned from sniffing at the shed and looked up at her, growling. She snatched her hand back. "Sorry. Daddy did say that."

The dog put his paws on Kiki's shoulders and licked her face. "Okay, okay. *Jah, Vohl,* you are a pussycat." She giggled.

"Look, Kiki, there's something stuck in here." Joan put a mittened hand against the shed's wall and pulled. "See?" She held up a tarnished chain with a bit of flat, dirty gold hanging from it.

"I think that's a menorah." Kiki squinted at the nine-pointed trinket. I've seen pictures of them."

CHAPTER FOUR

"Yuck! It's dirty!" Joan dropped the charm in Kiki's outstretched hand. "Probably belonged to the people who lived here before us. Don't go thinking it has anything to do with *Nazis*, just because it's Jewish."

Kiki ignored her, leaning down to rub Roland's ears. He looked up, shook bits of icy dirt off his nose, and sniffed the shed wall. "Whatcha doing, puppy?" She looked into his shining black eyes. *Do dogs have a sixth sense?*

"Let's go out front." Joan walked around the side of the house.

That was her plan all along, I bet. Kiki looked down at Roland chewing contentedly on a board. "Do we follow her or go back inside? Either way, I'm in trouble: you're not allowed in front, and I'm supposed to stay with Joan." Dropping the charm in her pocket, she ran after her sister.

At the house's stucco-and-stone front corner, Kiki stopped.

Joan stood on the curb, pretending to apply lipstick while watching two German boys across the lane. *I knew it.* Behind Kiki a window creaked open; she turned and saw Ilse, the new maid, looking down at them.

"Was ist los? Komm gleich, kinder! Schnell!"

From across the street the boys looked at Ilse, then grinned at Joan. *"Ach du Lieber, ein klienes baby!"* They burst out laughing.

Joan glared first at Ilse, then at the young *herrs.* She didn't see Roland come around the corner of the house until he lunged past her, snarling.

"Stop him!" Kiki screamed. She grabbed the trailing leash and was immediately yanked off her feet and dragged along the frozen ground.

"Roland! Halt," Joan shrieked. He stopped, ears down and growling. Across the street, the boys dropped their bundles of sticks and ran. Then, THUNK, the upstairs window closed.

Joan knelt next to Kiki. "Are you okay?"

"What do you think?" Kiki looked down at her bleeding, scraped knees.

"What in the world?" Mama stood in the front doorway, hands on hips. Ilse hovered behind her. "Kiki? Joan? Out in front with Roland against orders? Get in here immediately. I hope no one got hurt!"

Just me. Kiki got to her feet, trying not to cry. Her knees stung.

"He was going after some kids, Mama, but I called 'Halt' and he stopped." Joan sounded smug. "Isn't that great? He knows I'm his boss, just like Daddy."

"No, it is not great." Mama's chin jutted out angrily. "Get inside this instant. You'll both answer to your father for this. Kiki, look at your legs! Is that from playing in the dirty snow?"

Kiki groaned. "I wasn't playing, Mama. Roland dragged me. And I only took him out front because you said to always stay with Joan." Kiki's lower lip quivered. Her knees really stung.

Joan's eyes widened. She stared at Kiki and ran into the house.

"Stop right there, young ...." Mama's command was cut off by Ilse's,

"*Gott in Himmel, Frau* Moore! *Das ist eine kriegshund?* Is that a war dog?" There was fear in the woman's voice.

Mama pushed past Ilse. "*Komm in die kuche.* You too, Kiki." Ilse cast a last, wondering look at Roland and turned to follow Mama.

From within a corner of the foyer Joan appeared. "C'mon, Roland. Let's take Kiki upstairs and clean off those knees. Sorry you got hurt, kid." Roland, then Joan and a limping Kiki hurried up the stairs.

Sorry doesn't make it hurt any less. Kiki said nothing until they were in the bathroom with the door closed. "I thought Daddy was joking about Roland being trained to attack civilians. I believe it, now." She sat on the edge of the claw-footed tub and reached for a wash cloth. "Why would the Germans train dogs to attack their own people?"

"Who knows? Let's focus on your knees. Dirt and blood—so icky!" Joan gave Kiki what, for her, was a friendly smile.

From downstairs voices floated up—Mama's, then Ilse's. "I wish I knew German," Kiki whispered. "It sounds like they're arguing."

Joan nodded. "Let's stay out of their way for a while, okay? Give Mama time to cool off. Maybe if we get our homework done, she won't be mad anymore."

As they left the bathroom, Ilse's knot of blond hair appeared in the downstairs hallway. The girls dashed to their room and Kiki closed the door, pushing the lock button. Almost immediately the doorknob rattled and **Rap, Rap,** sounded on the solid wood door. "You will, *bitte,* study the *Deutsch.* I help."

Kiki and Joan looked at each other. Joan groaned. She put her mouth close to the door and called, "Yes. I mean, *Ja*. We will study, but we don't need help."

The hallway was silent. Roland went to the door and sniffed along the bottom, then came back and lay down next to the bed.

Kiki stage-whispered, "Is she gone?" Joan put a finger to her lips. When they heard the stairs creak, both girls relaxed.

"I wish she'd go away forever." Joan's lower lip pushed out in a frown. Mama's been a nervous wreck since we got that *fräulien*. She won't do anything Mama asks, and have you noticed how silly Daddy is around her?"

Kiki nodded. "Poor Mama. It's like Daddy has a crush on Ilse!"

Half-an-hour later—Joan sat writing in a notebook while Kiki read a *Nancy Drew* book—Mama called through the door, "I'm going out, girls."

Joan stood and quickly opened the door. "You look lovely, Mama."

Mrs. Moore, beautiful in her red wool coat with the fox fur stole, frowned. "I expect you to behave properly. Don't give Ilse any trouble." Her mascaraed eyes filled with worry. When neither girl spoke, she left the room.

Kiki's lower lip trembled. "We don't give Ilse trouble. She finds it all by herself. Doesn't Mama get that?"

"I guess not." Joan's shoulders drooped. "Ilse probably thinks we should be shot for taking Roland in the front yard. I hate this place!"

"Maybe we caused trouble for Daddy. Maybe he'll be court martialed or something." Kiki sat down next to the dog and scratched between his ears. "What's your story, big boy?"

When the old grandfather clock downstairs chimed six, Ilse

appeared in the girls' doorway. *"Schnell zeit zum essen."* Dinnertime.

"Okay. *Ja. Danka shon."* Kiki and Joan filed silently out of the room and down the stairs. When they were seated at the kitchen table, Ilse ladled Mama's potato soup from the tureen and gave each girl a piece of brown bread. *"Du bist geschin spulin."* Wash up after yourselves. Ilse pointed to the sink and left the kitchen. At the sound of feet on the staircase, Kiki smiled. "We don't have to eat with her. Hooray."

"We have to do the dishes, though." Joan shrugged. "That's what *'geschin spulin'* means."

"Did you notice how she avoided Roland?" Kiki slipped a piece of bread under the table, smiling when the dog grabbed it.

"She always does. You just never noticed." Joan scraped up a last drop of soup.

"Are you still mad at me?" Kiki talked through a bite of bread. "You shouldn't be. All I did was tell the truth."

Joan pushed away from the table and went to the stove, checking the simmering teakettle. "I know. You can't help being a tattletale any more than I can help being a tortured teenager." She sighed.

"What do you mean, tortured?" Kiki watched as her sister poured hot water into the dishpan, stirring it to melt the soap.

"You'll understand in a few years. Being in a strange country with no friends, that's torture." She rubbed the dishrag vigorously against the plates and bowls.

Kiki took the washed dishes from the drainer and dried them. "I'm tortured, too," she said. "Just not the same way as you. I'm scared all the time, and nobody understands me."

Joan did a thorough job of wiping down the table top, then tipped out the wash and rinse pans, "You just **think** no one understands you. Tell you what: I'll try to feel less tortured, and you try to be less weird." She gave Kiki a brilliant, phony smile. "And put a lid on that Nazi stuff, okay?"

"I'll try, but no promises." Kiki hung the towel on the rod at the end of the counter. A few minutes later, settled in the front room next to the radio, she whispered, "What were Mama and Ilse arguing about?"

"Us, probably." Joan looked surprised at the question. "Ilse's a German. They all hate us, even if they do need our help recovering from the war. Hitler fed them a lot of junk about how superior they are. They probably still believe it. Cleaning up after two American brats? Not easy for a proud Viking maiden." She reached over to turn up the radio's volume knob.

"I wish she wasn't here. She's so bossy!" Kiki's shoulders drooped.

Joan walked to the stairs, looked up to the dark second-story landing, and came back to stand in front of Kiki. "Want to teach her a lesson? Show her what happens when she disrespects us?"

Kiki sat up straight. "Is this something I'll have to tattle about?"

Joan's smile disappeared. "Nope." She looked away from Kiki. "Forget I said anything. As long Daddy's on Ilse's side, we don't have a chance."

"What do you mean? You think he'll get rid of Roland?"

Joan's eyebrows went up. "Roland? I hope not. He's our only friend. No, we need to make Daddy think Roland's no problem to Ilse or anyone else, and we need to behave ourselves. It's Mama I worry about. She was better off when there was an ocean between her and Daddy. At least then she didn't have to compete with the *fräuleins*." A door opened in the upstairs hall. "Shhh!" Joan put a finger to her lips. "It's almost time for I Love a Mystery. Turn up the radio."

Later—Kiki was already under the covers and half-asleep—Joan leaned on one elbow and whispered, "How come you ran like crazy out of the back yard? Did you see another ghost?"

Kiki shivered. She glanced up at Joan. "Thanks for reminding me, just when I'm going to sleep. Now I'll probably have nightmares." She punched her pillow and turned away.

"So, is that a yes? You saw a ghost? Tell me about it. A Nazi soldier? One of the people who used to live here?" Joan chuckled. "I think I'll write about you for that essay the teacher assigned us."

Kiki curled up under the covers, her back to Joan. *What did I do to deserve her for a sister, God? You could have given me anyone, and you chose her.*

Much later, around midnight, a noise woke Kiki. She peered around the moonlit room, realizing she'd heard a door open out in the hall. *Mama and Daddy coming home? No. They came in a while ago; Daddy's noisy after an evening at the Officer's Club.*

She slipped from under the covers, grabbed her robe and tiptoed to the bedroom door. Caution—unusual for Kiki—prevailed and she opened the door just a crack. The upstairs hall was empty, but the door to the attic stairs was slightly open. *Did Ilse come down, maybe to use the bathroom? No. There's no light on in there.*

"C-r-reak." Downstairs, the front door protested at being pulled open in the twenty-degree night. The rush of cold air brought a muttered, *"Gott in Himmel."* Then the door clicked shut.

Kiki tiptoed across the upstairs landing and looked out the small circular window onto the porch and front steps. In the moonlight she could see a heavily bundled figure hurry through the front gate and down the street. It could have been Mama in the coat, scarf and skirts except that, as the figure turned the corner, the scarf slipped down and a knot of blond hair reflected the moonlight.

Where is Ilse going in the middle of the night?

CHAPTER FIVE

"Kiki? What the hell are you doing out of bed? It's two o'clock in the morning!" Daddy stood in the bedroom doorway, peering at his daughter through bloodshot eyes.

"Oh, uh ...." Kiki thought fast. "Nothing. I heard a noise." She scampered back across the hall and into bed.

"Stay there. I don't want you wandering around the house at night." Daddy's voice was slurred. He sounded tired; tired and angry. He pulled the girls' bedroom door closed and Kiki heard the shuffle of his receding footsteps.

The next morning Kiki was half-way through her Cream of Wheat before she remembered Ilse leaving the house after midnight. Studying her mother's profile—Mama stood at the stove, serenely stirring the hot cereal—Kiki wondered, *Should I ask her about it? No. She'd say it's none of my business. And it might get me in trouble again.*

"Fall out, girls." Daddy opened the front door and stuck his head in.

"Yes, sir." The girls pushed away from the table and hurried to the front hall, slipped on their parkas and ran outside.

As Kiki climbed into the Jeep Mama called from the porch, "You forgot your bookbag, Kiki!" She held up Kiki's bulky camo knapsack.

Kiki looked in the rearview mirror, saw Colonel Moore's black eyes looking coldly back at her. She bolted from the Jeep, grabbed the knapsack and jumped back in as her father shifted gears and drove onto *Viersträusse*.

The drive to school was short and silent. Joan and Kiki knew better than to chatter when Daddy chauffeured them after a late night at the Officers' Club. Joan spent the ten minutes studying her reflection in a compact mirror, finger-brushing her front teeth. Kiki stared out through the side flap.

Where did Ilse go last night? Did Daddy send her away? Am I in trouble because I saw them? She glanced at the back of her fathers' neck; his black hair was hidden under the olive-green cap. *Should I talk to him, ask about Roland and that gold charm?*

"Uh, Daddy?"

Colonel Moore glanced in the rearview mirror.

"I hope we didn't get you in trouble--you and Roland. We won't have to give him up, will we? He's a nice dog. I'll be really careful not to let him out in front again." Kiki's voice ended in a squeak.

Colonel Moore said nothing, but his jaw set menacingly. Joan, startled out of admiring her teeth, gave a nervous giggle. "We know he's your dog, not ours, Daddy. He knows it, too. We won't even take him in the back yard again if you say."

For the first time in Kiki's memory, her father sighed. Then he reached into a pocket and drew out a half-smoked cigar. He clamped it between his teeth. "Roland's not going anywhere," came out muffled. "You two will, though, if you don't clean up your act."

Kiki and Joan glanced at one another, then looked quickly away as the Jeep stopped in front of the American dependents' school. They scrambled out and ran up the building's wide marble steps, joining students huddled outside the carved wooden door. Kiki waved goodbye to the Jeep's cloud of exhaust at the corner.

The school occupied one room on the ground floor of a many-columned marble building. According to Mama, the building resembled the Napa County Courthouse. The interior, even more grand than the outside, had wide marble floors, crystal chandeliers, and statues of naked people hovering tactfully in corners. A school day in Bad Kissengen bore little resemblance to Kiki's stateside experience. According to Joan, it was more like a high school study hall. The students worked on assignments from their Stateside schools while Miss Rose, the attractive brunette teacher, flirted with the officers.

Kiki walked up the steps, her thoughts on Colonel Moore and the night before. *Was it just a coincidence, Daddy and Ilse both up last night? Did she leave because of Roland? She and Mama argued yesterday; maybe she won't come back.* Buoyed by that thought, Kiki hurried along the corridor.

"Did you study for the quiz, Kiki?" Harold Brown, a freckle-faced fourteen-year-old with curly red hair and perennially fogged-up glasses, held open the classroom door.

"*Ja,* a little. Did you?" Kiki dropped her knapsack to the floor next to the conference table. "Let's go over the words." The quiz was on counting in German, the only subject Miss Rose actually taught. "I'll say them, you write them, then we'll switch."

Harold got paper and pencil from his knapsack and dropped into a chair. "Go."

"Eins, zwei, drei, vier, funf, sechs, sieben, acht, neun, zehn." Kiki waited for Harold to finish writing the numbers from one to ten in German. Then, "Elf, zwolf, dreizehn, vierzehn, funfzehn, sechszehn, siebzehn, achtzehn, neunzehn, zwanzig," Thirteen to twenty rolled easily off her tongue.

When he finished writing, he looked up. "You really have the accent down."

Kiki blushed. She wasn't used to compliments. "Let's switch. You read. I'll write."

Walking down the building's marble steps after school with Joan a few steps ahead, Kiki heard, "You're surprised she knows the language? You wouldn't be if you had to live with her. She's obsessed with this place. Sees Nazis around every corner."

Humiliation flooded Kiki. She turned and walked sideways along the bottom step, stopping at the corner of the building. *What do I do? No way can I ride home in the car pool with them.* She let her knapsack drop onto the steps and slumped down next to it. As she sat there, knees up and face down, she heard, "Uh, Kiki?"

She lifted her head enough to see Harold's faded corduroy trousers at her eye level.

"C'mon. My mom's waiting for us." Harold's voice was soft. When she looked up, Kiki saw the freckles standing out below his anxious brown eyes. She swiped at her snotty nose and got silently to her feet.

"What's wrong? Joan's big mouth hurt your feelings?" Harold sounded disgusted. "Brush it off. Not exactly fun, having a kid sister who's smarter **and** prettier." He grinned. "Give the old girl some slack."

A giggle rose up through Kiki's tears. "You're crazy, Harold!" She picked up the knapsack and trudged across the gravel to Mrs. Brown's Jeep.

On the ride home Joan kept her back to Kiki, even though they and two other kids were squeezed together in the Jeep's back seat. It wasn't until they were in the house and hanging up their coats that Joan managed a curt, "Sorry."

Kiki ignored her.

"I told Harold and the others we'd explore the Black Forest with them this afternoon. It'll be more fun if you aren't pouting." The sly grin on Joan's face made her look like the Cheshire cat. She turned away, calling, "We're home, Mama. Mama?"

From the kitchen they heard a stern, "*Guten tag, kinder.*"

"I forgot." Joan groaned. "Mama went somewhere with Daddy."

Kiki glanced warily toward the kitchen. There, dead center on the kitchen table, was a note in Mama's spidery, precise handwriting:

Joan and Kiki, Ilse is in charge until your father and I return tomorrow. I expect you to give her your complete cooperation.

"Sit, *bitte.*" Ilse's arms were folded against her bosom. "You will the snack *essen.*" She placed two apples on the table.

Kiki took a step toward the table. Joan, though, picked up an apple and walked out of the kitchen, calling back, "We're going to the Browns' *haus* to study."

"*Herr* General Brown?" At the mention of the Base Commander, Ilse's voice softened.

"Ja," Kiki hurried after Joan, not daring to look back at the maid.

When they got to the front door Roland—he'd been asleep on his mat—got to his feet. "Wish we could take you with us, boy." Kiki gave his head a quick pat as she left.

It was a short walk to the Browns' house; Bad Kissengen was a small village, after all. Kiki didn't know the way--Joan was better acquainted with the town--so she followed along, jumping from cobblestone to cobblestone and noticing landmarks. *That cottage has a thatched roof and a blue door; There's a wheelbarrow next to that tree; there's one of those roadside shrines Mama likes.* When her sister glanced back, Kiki hurried to catch up.

"Did you know the fairy tales in your big book are set in the Black Forest? The guy who wrote them must have been from around here." Joan chattered as if Kiki wasn't mad at her.

"Makes sense," Kiki muttered. "Hans Christian Anderson is a German name."

"*Ja.*" Joan giggled. "I'm glad we're not going into the forest alone. In case we pull a Hansel and Gretel and, you know, meet the Big Bad Wolf."

"Those stories were written a long time ago. Do wolves still exist? Around here, I mean." Kiki shivered. She looked behind her at the meandering path next to the street.

Joan sneered. "There you go again. Scaredy cat! Grow up, will you?"

Kiki's shoulders drooped. "Cut it out. You know how I am." She felt like turning around and going home. *Who's worse, Joan or Ilse?*

"Right," Joan grumbled. "I do know. But, do **you** know how irritating it is? Why can't you be normal, like me?"

Kiki pushed past her and kept walking. When she saw Harold waving to them from a porch half a block away, she made an effort to unclench her fists. *At least Harold likes me. Joan can go fly a kite.*

When they reached the Browns' house, Harold studied their faces and grinned. "You two still scrapping? Call a time out for the rest of the day, will you?"

Before either girl could answer Peggy, Harold's long-legged sixteen-year-old sister, came out of the house, her red ponytail swinging. "Did you get the flashlight, little brother?" Without waiting for an answer Peggy turned to Joan. "Is this your first time in the Black Forest? You'll love it. We've gone with the folks a few times. Our mom was a Girl Scout Leader back home, so of course when we got here, we had to do a nature walk." Peggy strode down the steps, linked arms with Joan, and looked back at Harold and Kiki. "C'mon, little ones!"

"Yes, sir, sergeant, sir." Harold winked at Kiki. "Bossy big sisters: Adapt or perish, kid."

They followed the older girls along the street to a stand of trees marking the outskirts of *Schwarzwald*, the Black Forest. Kiki began to relax. Even in faraway Napa, California, the Black Forest was famous. The home of Grimm's Fairy Tales, it was known to children the world over for Cinderella, Sleeping Beauty, wicked witches, and many other characters. She gazed into the dark canopy of evergreen trees, mossy tree trunks and dense brambles, wondering at their almost human shapes. She shivered. "This place is spooky."

Harold nodded. "Those witches in the fairy tales— remember the one where a witch lured Hansel and Gretel into her gingerbread house? They were real. They lived here, in the Black Forest."

Kiki's eyes widened. "The houses around here are decorated like gingerbread!"

He nodded knowingly. "I read up on it when we first got here. There were lots of witches in Germany in the Middle Ages, especially in *Schwarzwald*." Harold looked expansive, like he enjoyed being the authority. "Legend has it this place is home to werewolves, too; even the devil."

Kiki tried to smile. "Black magic in the Black Forest? Maybe that's where Nazis came from." She looked down at the sandstone path. "Let's change the subject. When you know me better, you'll know I scare easy." She braved a moment's eye contact. "Sorry you heard Joan and me bickering. Back home in Napa, where we didn't have to be at the same school, we got along better. My weirdness didn't affect her so much."

"You don't seem weird to me. Sensitive, but that's a good

thing." Harold picked up a pine cone and threw it into the branches of a tree. A cloud of yellow pollen immediately rose up into a streak of sunlight. Then, from somewhere deep in the forest they heard, **Cuckoo! Cuckoo!**

All four kids stopped. "Oh my gosh, I thought cuckoos only existed in clocks!" Joan sounded awed.

"This place feels magical," Kiki whispered. "Cold, though."

The path Peggy led them on was clear of snow, as was the ground beneath the trees. When Kiki looked up through the towering firs, she saw streaks of white along the branches. "So pretty," she whispered. "Brrrr."

"This must be where those old women get the bundles of wood they carry." Joan picked up a twig lying on the path. "I guess they're used to the cold."

They'd been walking in the forest for half an hour when Peggy stopped. "Look, Harold; through those trees; it's that cabin Dad wouldn't let us go near."

"*Ja vol.*" Harold stepped off the path and disappeared, then reappeared close to a dark, mossy rectangular shape. "Spooky," he called, grinning.

"C'mon. We can't let him have all the fun!" Peggy, then Joan and Kiki pushed in through the low-growing bushes.

The cabin was made of moss-covered wood and ancient stones. It blended so well with its' surroundings, Kiki had to squint to realize it was man-made. "You think anyone lives here?" *It **is** kind of spooky. We shouldn't be here.*

"There's no smoke coming out of the chimney." Joan stepped up and rattled the cabin's door handle.

"I don't see any footprints." Peggy squinted at the ground like a seasoned tracker.

"If your father said not to be here…." Kiki shivered. When

the others ignored her she walked to the back of the cabin, trying to breathe through her fear like Daddy had taught her. Down close to the foundation stones on the rear wall she noticed a small knot hole. *What's that?*

"Guys," she called, "Come see this."

"What'd you find?" Harold got there first and knelt next to her. "I'm surprised that's not plugged up."

"What's the big deal, Kiki?" Joan giggled. "It's a knot hole. Maybe they left it open for a pet mouse."

"Can you see inside?" Peggy squatted next to her brother.

Harold put a hand over the hole. "Kiki found it. She gets the first look."

Peggy and Joan sat back, frowning. Kiki got on her hands and knees and put an eye to the knot hole, then jumped back, horrified. "An eye! I saw an eye! Someone looked back at me!"

"Wait. What?" Peggy's voice had the tone of a Girl Scout Leader again. "You saw an eye?" She knelt and looked in the knot hole, then drew back. "What color? Black? Because the one I saw was green."

Kiki nodded. "Black. *Ja.*" She suddenly understood. "Your eyes are green, Peggy."

"They've blocked the hole with a mirror. Someone has a mean sense of humor." Peggy frowned.

"I almost wet my pants." Kiki looked at Harold, saw him trying not to laugh, and giggled.

"Tell you what." Joan sounded unimpressed. "I'm going to poke that mirror out of the way and get a look inside." She grabbed a stick and jammed it through the knot hole, then squinted into the opening.

"What do you see?"

"An empty room. Maybe a table." Joan stood and brushed the dirt off her skirt. "You want another look, Kiki, now the mirror's gone?"

"Okay." Kiki knelt and put her eye to the hole again. When

her vision adjusted to the shadowy interior, she gasped. She saw a table, as Joan said. However: standing by the table were a woman, a man, and a little boy, holding onto one another and softly weeping.

CHAPTER SIX

Kiki got to her feet and stepped back from the cabin wall. "Someone's in there," she whispered. "We need to get out of here."

"What? I didn't see anyone." Joan bent down for another look.

"It's my turn." Harold pushed past the girls and put an eye to the knothole.

"Let's just go." Peggy sounded nervous. "Our dads will get in trouble if we're caught trespassing." She stepped back, away from the cabin.

"She's right. Let's go." Harold got to his feet.

"But ...." Joan stared hard at Kiki for a second, then grabbed her arm and called, "Wait for us!"

After a few minutes of panicked crashing through the underbrush, Peggy called the group to a halt. They listened for pursuers, hearing only the sounds of the winter forest: the 'plop' of snow falling from a branch, a far-off "**Cuckoo, Cuckoo**," a blue jay's squawk.

Kiki lagged behind, her mind on the people in the cabin. *Were they real? Did Harold see them? I can't ask, in case he didn't. What if I'm seeing ghosts again, like in Napa? There were no signs anyone was there: no smoke from the chimney, no footprints in the snow, no sound from inside the cabin.*

"Kiki, keep up!" Joan's waspish tone got the younger girl's attention.

"Okay, okay.".

When they reached the waterfall—their path dead-ended at a cliff camouflaged by thick fir trees—they heard the water before they saw it.

"If there ever was a guard rail, it's long gone." Peggy pushed aside tree branches and got very quiet. "There it is." She turned to Harold. "Step back so the girls can see."

Across a steep gorge frothy water tipped over a cliff, thundered past rock outcroppings and plunged down, down into an ice-encrusted pool. As Joan and Kiki stared, a double rainbow appeared in the mist.

"Somethin', isn't it?" Harold sounded expansive, like the waterfall was his personal property. "I plan to go swimming here next summer."

"It's off limits," Peggy frowned. "According to our dad."

"Oh, my gosh! Those rainbows! Thank you so much for bringing us here," Joan gushed. She nudged Kiki.

"Yeah," Kiki nodded. "This is really beautiful."

They started on the trail home, Harold hanging back to walk with Kiki. "You okay about that creepy cabin?"

Kiki shook her head.

"Did you really see people? All I saw was a table."

Can I tell him the truth? She stared at the muddy ground. *I don't want to lie. He's been so nice to me.*

She waited until Peggy and Joan were farther along the trail before saying, "My mind plays tricks on me sometimes, Harold. I had that problem in Napa, too. It runs in my family."

"That's tough." Harold frowned. "You ever need to talk to someone ...." He straightened his shoulders. "Let's pick up our pace before my sister yells at us. I've had all I can take of Park Ranger Peggy."

Kiki hurried after him. "Do you think the Germans' suffering is our fault? Us Allies, I mean?"

Harold looked startled. "No way," he blurted. "They did it to themselves—well, not the Jews and everyone else the Nazis murdered." He glanced at her. "You know my family's Jewish, right?" He turned away, walking fast down the path.

Kiki stood still, watching him go. *They're Jewish? Huh. I thought it was hard for me, being here. Must be way harder for him; he could be related to some of these restless spirits.* She went slowly along the path, her thoughts on what little she knew about the Nazis. *When I said I see things, did he know I was talking about ghosts?*

She looked around, saw an edge of the cabin's deeply-pitched roof between the trees, and felt suddenly vulnerable. The pristine beauty of the area, so impressive just minutes ago, now had an ominous edge. A sense of danger ran along Kiki's spine and she bolted like a startled deer, frantic to catch up with the others.

Winter days were short in *Deutschland*. It was almost dark when Joan and Kiki walked up *Vierstrausse* to their house. "Look, there's the Jeep. Weren't Mama and Daddy supposed to be out this evening?" Joan ran up the front steps. "I hope we're not in trouble. We left without telling anyone."

Joan's hand was on the front doorknob when the door opened and Colonel Moore scowled at them. "Where the hell have you two been? I was about to call the MPs." He stepped back. "Get in here, right now!"

"Yes, sir." The girls pushed through the doorway, elbowing each other as they avoided his heavy hand. Kiki looked toward the kitchen, hoping to see Mama. Instead, Ilse stood by the sink, grinning. *She must have told on us. That's why Daddy's so mad.*

"Komm her, kinder! Ilse's tone was revoltingly sweet.

"We went for a walk with the Brown kids, Daddy." Joan talked fast, almost spraying out the words. "We would've told the *fraulein,* but she wasn't here. No one was here."

Where's Mama?" Kiki's voice squeaked.

Daddy looked at Ilse, then at his daughters. He shook his head. "Go to your room, both of you. You ever pull a stunt like that again, you'll regret it." As they started up the stairs he added, "Your mother's due back by 0600."

The girls hadn't been in their room ten minutes when the door opened and Ilse looked in. *"Komme, hilf in der kuche.* Come help in the kitchen." She added, sounding triumphant, *"Der* Colonel went out, but he'll be back."

From her spot on the floor next to the bed, Kiki stared up at Ilse, not moving. "Come on." Joan slid off the bed, nudged Kiki with her foot and hurried from the room.

"Wait for me!" Kiki put down the list of words she'd been studying and followed them.

Ilse began barking orders before the girls were even off the stairs. *"Settenze den tisch,* Kiki." Set the table. "Joan, *schneide das brot. "* Slice the bread.

"Are you eating with us? Uh, *Du bist essen* with us?" Kiki

forced a polite tone of voice, thinking, *I hope not.* She reached for four plates.

"No." Ilse shook her head. *"Herr Colonel auch nicht."* Not the Colonel, either.

The girls watched warily as Ilse took a cup from the dish cabinet and poured coffee into it, then took a sip. She glanced at the girls, smirking. *"Herr* Colonel say, *Yah vohl."* She set the cup gently on the wooden drainboard and stepped into the rationed-goods pantry.

In a flash Joan was at the drainboard, salt shaker in hand. She shook it over the steaming coffee, then retreated to the table. A minute later Ilse emerged from the pantry, a spoonful of sugar balanced carefully in her hand.

"Guten Aben, kinder." Good night, children. Ilse tipped the sugar into the coffee, picked up the cup and left the kitchen.

Kiki stared at her sister, trying to process what she'd just seen: salt in coffee? She'd never had coffee, but she was pretty sure salt wasn't a good idea.

"Why'd you ….? Oh. I get it. To ruin her treat." She nodded knowingly.

Joan slid onto a chair and served herself a portion of Mama's chicken stew. "What salt? Are you seeing things again? Nobody put salt in any coffee." She smiled. "Sit down. Let's eat."

BANG! Far above them in the attic someone slammed a door, hard. Then feet stomped down the stairs and Ilse, her face contorted with rage, appeared in the kitchen doorway. *"Du bist schweinehunds, du verfault Amerikanisch!"* You are pigdogs, you rotten Americans!

Kiki dropped into a chair, staring at the enraged *fraulein.* "Joan," she whispered. "Do something."

"I, er …." Joan stuttered.

"Gott in Himmel!" Ilse turned away, her eyes sprouting tears. She went slowly back up the stairs.

Kiki waited until she heard an upstairs door close before hissing, "Weren't we in enough trouble? You had to ruin her precious coffee?"

Joan said nothing. She was smiling, though, and trying not to laugh. Kiki folded her arms in a replica of Mama. "What in the world? Explain yourself, young lady!"

"She deserved it. That and a lot more! Get a clue, Kiki. She's trying to take Daddy away from us." Joan gulped back hiccups.

Kiki was staggered. It felt as though she'd been slapped. She managed to whisper, "What … what do you mean?"

"Oh, grow up." Joan's tone dripped with disgust. "Haven't you heard them tiptoeing around at night, giggling? It's so gross."

"But …but … we came all this way to take care of Daddy." Kiki was stunned. She had no concept of life without her father. "Is he going to leave us?"

Joan took a bite of bread. "I don't know. I hope not."

"How do we stop her? Besides ruining the coffee, I mean."

Joan sighed. "Maybe talk to Daddy? Let him know how much we love him?"

"Talk? Are you kidding? He never, ever listens to us." Kiki frowned. "That's nothing new, though. You know how he says we're in the way, that we're nuisances? I wish he thought Ilse was a nuisance."

Joan looked thoughtful. She popped the last bit of bread in her mouth and mumbled, "Let's do the dishes. Maybe a plan will come to us. She stood and carried her plate to the sink. "You wash. I'll dry."

"I wonder when Mama's coming home." Kiki tried not to whine, but it was hard. She and Joan had done first their chores, then their homework. Now, they were getting ready for bed. "Where'd she go, anyway?"

"How would I know?" Joan's grumpiness, Kiki had learned, meant she was scared. "Maybe she's playing bridge with the officer's wives. No, that can't be. She's been gone all day. Oh," Joan continued, "why aren't we back in Napa, where there are no *frauleins*?"

"Why aren't we anywhere besides here!" Kiki climbed into bed, trying not to cry.

Joan turned out the light and got under the covers on her side of the bed. "Maybe I'm wrong. Maybe there's nothing going on between Daddy and that *fraulein.*"

"You really think so?" Kiki gulped. "Mama has never stayed away all day before, though. And Daddy's grumpier than ever; he even swore at Roland yesterday."

From Joan's side of the bed there was a muffled, "Good night, Kiki."

"Wait a sec. I forgot to show you something." Kiki stuck an arm out from under the blanket and patted the top of the nightstand. "I polished that trinket you found by the shed."

Joan switched on the light and took the gold charm from Kiki. "Nice." She handed it back and turned off the light.

"It's Jewish."

"What?" Joan sounded sleepy. "What'd you say?"

"Jewish. It's a Menorah. For Hanukkah. I've seen pictures of them."

"Oh. Night, Kiki." Joan's words tapered off into light, nasal breathing.

Kiki slid the charm under her pillow and rested her cheek against the down-filled cloth. *It's a reminder to me to say my prayers.* As she drifted off to sleep, murmuring, "God, bless me and Joan, Mama and Daddy, Roland ...." the German shepherd popped into Kiki's head. *Where is he? I haven't seen him all day.* She nudged Joan. "Psst! Where's Roland?"

Joan groaned and buried her head under the pillow.

The next morning, when Kiki stumbled sleepily into the kitchen for breakfast Mama was there, serenely stirring oatmeal.

"Mama!" Kiki threw her arms around her mother and held on tight.

"My goodness! What brought that on?" Mama's voice was gentle. She returned Kiki's hug with a half-hug of her own.

As Kiki stepped shyly back, she saw Roland lying next to the table. "Roland! Was he with you, Mama? Where'd you go?"

Joan slipped into a chair at the table. "Yes, Mama. We were worried about you."

"Roland and I went on an errand for your father." Mama sounded nervous. "Thank you for worrying." She paused. "I need to talk to you about yesterday: you were rude to Ilse and you played a cruel trick on her."

"But, Mama," Joan squeaked. "We ...."

"Quiet. No excuses. Ilse is not just a maid; she's a citizen of the country where we're guests." Mama squared her shoulders, her expression serious. "Your father and I put her in charge. By disobeying her, you disobeyed us."

"We thought ...." Kiki whispered.

"You thought? Hasn't your thinking gotten you in enough trouble, Kiki? You are the least qualified of any of us to be thinking on your own!"

Kiki looked down at her feet. Mama's words hurt more than Daddy's belt.

"Eat your breakfast and go to school. I want you to think, all day, about how your mean tricks hurt not just Ilse, but your father and me, too." Mama set two bowls of cereal on the table and strode from the kitchen.

Kiki looked at Joan, saw tears on her sister's cheeks, and put down her spoon. "I'm not hungry anymore." She pushed away from the table and went slowly upstairs.

As they walked up the steps to school, Kiki squeezed the charm she'd put in her coat pocket, then touched Joan's arm. This took courage; Joan usually preferred that Kiki act like they weren't related. "Do you still think we should be worried about Ilse? Mama doesn't seem to be."

Joan shook off Kiki's hand. "More than ever." She stopped and looked hard at her sister. "Don't breathe a word of this to anyone, you hear me?"

As if I'd blab the family business to other military kids. Kiki went to her seat at the conference table and folded her hands.

"I have a treat for you today, students. Two of my lieutenant friends are taking us on a walking field trip to the Bad Kissengen cemetery." Miss Rose blushed pinker than her name.

CHAPTER SEVEN

The Bad Kissengen cemetery on this winter day was a cold and dreary place. Mossy stuff hung from the branches of leafless trees, the sandy soil was wet and gritty, and statues carved from the area's granite hillsides tilted precariously in all directions.

Luckily for the thirteen chilled teenagers, the cemetery was less than a mile from the school building. Miss Rose and her lieutenants led the way, the students following in straggling twos and threes. Kiki walked with the only other sixth-grader, a sturdily built girl named Jacquie who had her nose in a Bad Kissengen guidebook.

When they reached an arched gate embellished by wrought-iron crosses, angels, and cherubim, Miss Rose clapped her mittened hands together. "We're here!" She sounded almost surprised. "Be sure to take notes, class. There'll be an essay assignment tonight."

"Does the guidebook have cemeteries, Jacquie?" Kiki peered over her companion's shoulder.

The girl looked up, stared uncomprehendingly at Kiki for a second, then shook her head. "Maybe. The book is in German. There aren't many pictures." She gave Kiki a vacant smile and walked away.

Guess I'm on my own. Please God, don't let me stumble over any ghosts. Kiki looked back at the entrance gates, noting the wrought-iron nameplate:

St. Boniface - Interglot 574

The weathered copper figure of a bearded man, a cross in one hand and a sword in the other, stood out against the wrought-iron. He seemed to stare intently at Kiki.

He looks mean. I don't want to meet his ghost, even if he is a saint. Is that sword real? Kiki stepped over to the gate, reached out and ran a mittened finger along the sword's edge.

Huh! She pulled her hand back, staring at a cut in her mitten. Blood trickled out.

"Did that sword cut you?" Harold Brown stood just behind Kiki. He sounded surprised.

Kiki looked over her shoulder. "Yes. It shouldn't be sharp, should it? I mean, Lord knows how long that statue's been here." She turned to face him. "What does *interglot* mean?"

"Death date. If they put the statue up when he died, the sword would be ..." Harold paused, " ... at least fifteen hundred years old. It would be as dull as a butter knife by now."

"Maybe it's not the original sword." Kiki pressed her fingers together to stop the bleeding. "Don't tell Miss Rose, please. I don't want to be in trouble again."

As if the teacher had heard her name, Miss Rose appeared from behind a mossy stone figure. "Does anyone know what identifies this cemetery as Catholic?"

Jacquie looked up from the guidebook. "I know, Miss Rose. My family's Catholic, and St. Boniface is one of our saints. He's a big deal in *Deutschland* history." She gave Kiki a quick, prim smile.

Harold said, "Looks like part of the cemetery was bulldozed. See over there? Were the Nazis trying to get rid of Catholics?"

Miss Rose stared blankly at Harold. One of the lieutenants, a short, dark-haired man with bushy eyebrows, spoke up. "Good observation, kid. The Reich persecuted anyone not considered Aryan. Catholics weren't exempt." He looked across to the damaged section. "I think that section was for non-Catholics, though."

Kiki shivered. Although most of the cemetery was devoid of ghostly energy, the bulldozed section had wisps of haze floating along the ground, especially by a large, new-looking marble plaque. *Ghosts. They're hovering around that memorial.*

She jammed her fists into the pockets of her parka. When the cut finger came in contact with smooth, cool metal, the hurting stopped. *The Menorah charm. I forgot I put it in there. Too bad it won't magically heal my cut finger.* The tension in her shoulders lessened as she cradled the charm in her palm. *Maybe the ghosts, the Jewish ones, anyway, will leave me alone.*

When Miss Rose began lecturing about tombstone inscriptions, Harold rolled his eyes at Kiki and wandered off toward the bulldozed area.

Okay. I get it. With everyone else concentrating on the teacher, it was easy for Kiki to slip away. She hurried past row upon row of tombstones, catching up with Harold at the far end of the cemetery. He stood silently, his head bowed, by the marble plaque.

Is he praying? As she waited for him to finish Kiki noticed wisps of fog drifting toward her, drifting and gathering into human shapes. Forcing down the impulse to bolt, she whispered, "Harold? Can we please get out of here? Now?"

He looked up, his face full of pain. He turned and, in two

long strides, stood next to Kiki.

"Some spirits are still here." The words just tumbled out of Kiki's mouth. *Good grief. Did I really say that?* She wished she could disappear.

"I feel it, too." Harold looked around, then sputtered, "Hell's Bells, if I'd known we were going to see what the Nazis did to Jewish graves ... and they think one little memorial makes it all okay?" He took Kiki's arm, turned her around and almost dragged her back along the cemetery path. "I probably shouldn't have told you we're Jewish. Not my dad; just mom and my sister and me. I don't think the Base Commander knows. Keep it to yourself, will you?"

This took Kiki completely by surprise. *Why do they need to lie? It's okay to be Jewish, isn't it, if you're an American?* She opened her mittened fist and held up the Menorah charm. "You want this? I found it in our back yard. It's a Jewish candlestick." She blushed. *He knows that. I am so dumb!*

Harold stopped, staring at the charm. "You found that?" He picked it up and held it near his face, examining it. "Real gold; Came off a girl's bracelet." He put a hand on Kiki's shoulder. "You mind if I give this to my mom? She's been wondering if there were Jews here in Bad Kissengen."

"Go ahead. Don't tell her what we saw here, though."

Harold's eyebrows went up. "What? The bulldozing? Why not?"

Kiki looked away. *He didn't see the ghosts. I'm not in trouble after all.* "It was really sad." She tried to sound casual.

"Hey! Where'd everybody go?" Harold looked around. "Did you see them leave? How long were we over there, anyway?" He sounded a little scared.

"They're down there, at the corner, see? C'mon." Kiki broke into a run along the path to the street gate. "We can catch up. Miss Rose won't know we ditched." She hadn't finished speaking before Harold rushed past.

Kiki felt herself smiling. *This school is such a joke. Miss Rose doesn't know anything about conducting a field trip. Rule number one: keep track of your students.*

When they reached the end of the straggling line, Joan turned around. "Where on earth were you, Kiki? It is so typical of you to get lost. Just wait 'til I tell Mama!"

"Give her a break." Peggy stepped out of the line to walk with Harold. "Pretty grim sight beyond the fence, little brother?" She smiled at Kiki. "I'll let your mom know Miss Rose messed up, marching us out before you two got back."

"Thanks, Peggy." Kiki avoided looking at Joan. "We weren't lost. Harold wanted to see that other part. I did, too."

Harold nodded. He draped an arm around his sister's shoulder, saying nothing.

Joan looked from Kiki to Peggy and Harold. She shrugged. "I guess Mama's got enough on her mind without this."

They walked along in silence, bringing up the end of the line. Kiki took the opportunity to organize her thoughts, tucking away for later examination the events at the cemetery. It was a beautiful day, cold but bright. Houses and stores on these *strasses* were undamaged and well maintained, windows sparkling and curtains hanging precisely halfway down the glass. Germany, there and at that moment, felt benign.

"I'd like to see where you found that, uh, token, Kiki. Maybe Peggy and I could come by after school?" Harold's voice cracked.

"What token?" Joan glanced at Harold, then Kiki. "That gold charm?"

Joan continued, "Can you, Peggy, come over after school? I'm sure Mama won't mind." She sounded eager.

I'm not the only one who misses her friends back home.

Peggy nodded. She and Joan walked ahead, talking quietly. Kiki heard snatches of their conversation: something about *frauleins* and military attack dogs.

Is Joan telling our family secrets? Kiki hung back, letting the older girls get out of earshot before saying, "Do you have a German maid, Harold? Or a war dog?" *If Joan can talk about that stuff, I can, too.*

Harold looked startled, then glanced down at Kiki. "What'd you say?"

"German maids; you know, *frauleins*. We have one. She's awful."

"She's a war dog?"

Kiki smothered an embarrassed giggle. "No, silly. A *fraulein*."

"Oh." Harold grinned. "We have a dog. My father rescued her. "Schatzi. She's a peach."

"Ours is named Roland. He's mostly my dad's. He's not safe around civilians." Kiki looked up at Harold. "What about maids? Do you have one of those?"

Harold rolled his eyes. "You should've been at our house when the first maid showed up. Mom took one look at her and said *Nein*. Something about not needing the competition. That *f raulein* left, and the next day we got the one we have now." He grinned again. "My secret name for her is Hatchet Face. Mom took to her from the beginning."

"So, my mama could turn Ilse in on a different model, someone old and ugly who won't flirt with Daddy?" Kiki blushed. *Oh, boy. I've definitely said too much.*

"Sure. Have your mom talk to mine." Harold adopted a worldly-wise swagger. "Those *frauleins* chase after anything in uniform."

Back in the classroom Kiki chewed on her pencil, wondering how to write about the field trip without mentioning ghosts. When the dismissal bell rang, she hurriedly scribbled two paragraphs comparing the German cemetery with one in Napa. Finishing with, 'Germans really love statues,' she slipped her paper under the others on Miss Rose's desk and hurried outside.

When Joan and Kiki got home from school, Ilse met them on the front porch. *"Deine mutter ist weg. Du wirst deine schulaufgaben machen.* Your mother is out. You will do your homework now."* At the girls' blank faces she sputtered, 'Schulaufgaben. Schoolwork. Schnell.'

Both girls muttered, *"Ja, Ja."* As Ilse turned away Kiki added, "We don't have any *schulaufgaben,* Ilse. And some friends--*freundinnen*--are coming over in a little while."

Ilse looked fiercely at both girls, her eyebrows lowered and her mouth a straight, accusing line. *"Freundinnen? Hier? Frau* Moore say *nicht* about *zis."*

"She won't mind." Joan gave Kiki a warning look. "She knows *die eltern.* Their parents. General Brown works with Daddy."

Ilse looked suspiciously from one girl to the other, standing tall and staring down at them. When they didn't waiver—it was hard; she was, to Kiki, huge and menacing—she finally said, *"Ja vol.* But *neine essen.* No food."

Kiki was in the kitchen a few minutes later, looking for a snack, when she heard the click, click of toenails against linoleum. "Roland! Didn't you go to work with Daddy?" She knelt to give the big dog a hug. "Have you been stuck inside all day? Want to go out in the back yard? Play ball? Play *mit das kugel*?" Roland stood on his hind legs, licking Kiki's face. "I'll take that as a *Ja, ja!*"

Outside in the cold, fresh air a few minutes later, Kiki spent most of Roland's playtime prying the ball from his mouth. He loved chasing it, but didn't understand the logic of giving it back to be thrown again. She was shaking dog spittle off her mittens when she heard, "You sure you should be putting your hands between those teeth?" Harold stood on the back steps with Peggy and Joan.

Roland instantly dropped the ball, his luxurious brown and black hair standing up along his back. He growled, showing fangs. Kiki knelt and put a hand on his head. "Friends, Roland. Daddy's *freundinnen.* Stand down." She kept her voice soft, but firm. The growling subsided. Roland sat back, eyes locked on Peggy and Harold.

"*Gut. Das is gut.* Now, they're going to come slowly down the steps, Joan first. They'll walk over to the shed." Kiki kept her eyes on Roland. "You and I will go in the house." She stood and Roland got to his feet, standing tight against her leg. "*Gut.* Good boy."

Joan, Peggy and Harold—Kiki was very glad Harold knew to stay behind the girls, in the least aggressive spot—came slowly down the stairs.

"Aren't you overacting, Kiki?" Joan sounded nervous.

"Can't hurt." Peggy gave Kiki a tight smile.

Kiki walked Roland up to the kitchen door, held it open as he went inside, and shut it with a last "*Gut hund.*" Good dog.

"She is so dramatic," Joan sneered. "He's not really dangerous."

"You could've fooled me; German shepherd, trained by the Nazis? Nice work, Kiki." Harold's face lit up in a 100-watt grin.

"So," Peggy looked around the yard. "Where'd you find that charm?"

"Oh, yeah." Joan gave a relieved sigh. "Over there, at the

shed. I found it."

Harold stepped up to the shed and examined the lock. "What's in here? You guys use this for storage?"

"I don't think so." Kiki looked at Joan. "If Daddy used it before we got here, the lock would be new."

Joan nodded. "He never comes out back." She looked at Harold and Peggy, then pulled a small screwdriver from her pocket. "You want to look inside? Courtesy of our kitchen toolbox?"

"That's ours?" Kiki looked nervously back at the house. In an upstairs window the curtains moved slightly. "You better put it back."

"Maybe we shouldn't do this. We don't want to get you in trouble." Peggy sounded disappointed.

"Mama's not home right now." Kiki smiled. "We can't ask her permission. I bet she'd be fine with it if she knew it was for our friends." Kiki took the screwdriver from Joan and pushed it into the keyhole. Bits of rust fell out, but the lock didn't budge.

"I have a better idea." Harold took the screwdriver. "Okay to take out the screws?" He squared his shoulders and assumed a manly frown. "This'll be a piece of cake."

After a few minutes of pressure the frozen screws let go, one by one. When Harold inserted the screwdriver between the lock and the door, there was a loud **CLICK** and the lock came away in his hand. Joan reached past him, grabbed the handle and pulled the door open.

"Eeeww!" All four stepped away from the stale air drifting out. Kiki squeezed her eyes shut, opened them and gasped. The slightly blurred figure of a small child, a little boy, stood blinking in the sunlight next to Harold.

CHAPTER EIGHT

"Open the door all the way. I'm not going in there until it gets aired out." Joan was the first to speak.

"Good thinking. Whew! I bet this hasn't been opened in years!" Harold grabbed the top of the door and pulled it wide open.

"Uh, what about ....?" Kiki sputtered, staring at the child.

He was very young, not more than three years old; with his black hair and white skin, he could have passed for a member of the Moore family except for his piercing blue eyes. When they fixed on Harold, fear emanated from the small romper-clad frame.

"*He's afraid? Why?*" Kiki looked at Joan, Harold and Peggy. All were moving around, waving their hands in the air and laughing. *They can't see him! They don't know they're in the presence of a ghost.* She looked squarely at the child, whispering, "Don't be afraid. We won't hurt you."

The child looked puzzled. He frowned and shook his head. He doesn't understand English. Makes sense. He is—was—German.

"You can go first, Kiki." Joan looked at her sister, a strange expression on her carefully made-up face. "Something wrong?"

"*Wer bist du? Wo ist Vater?*" Who are you? Where's father? The child spoke shyly, with a slight lisp.

"Uh, give me a minute." Kiki shook her head at Joan. *What do I do? Ignore him and go in the shed with my friends?* She gave an involuntary shiver. *Lord knows what we'll find in there; skeletons, like I found in that attic in Napa?* "I've changed my mind, guys. Daddy should be the first to explore the shed." Kiki tried to keep from looking at the little boy.

Harold groaned. "You lost your nerve? Worst thing we'd find in there would be, maybe, black widow spiders." As he spoke the little boy drifted toward him, lifted a short, sturdy leg and kicked, hard.

"Ouch!" Harold stumbled, almost losing his balance. He looked around, his gaze settling on Peggy. "Why'd you do that?" He bent down and rubbed his leg, then started toward the back stairs. The little boy, triumph shining from his small face, turned and drifted back into the shed.

Joan grabbed Kiki's arm. "Did you do something?" she hissed. "Peggy wasn't anywhere near him."

Kiki shook off Joan's hand. "Let's go back inside. Ilse's watching us."

"I was looking forward to doing some exploring." Peggy stood on the kitchen steps and looked longingly across the yard. "Maybe it was a bomb shelter. A lot of the people around here had them, you know. Especially at the end."

At that moment an upstairs window creaked open. Ilse called, "*Was iss los?*" What's the matter? "*Komm rein, schnell!*" Come inside immediately!

Harold stepped back onto the mud, looked up and called.

"*Ja vol, mein fraulein.*" He sounded disgusted.

"Sorry," Joan said to Peggy. "I didn't figure on Ilse. Or my chicken-livered sister."

"Yeah," Kiki mumbled. "Sorry." She glanced at the shed, then followed the others into the house. In the late afternoon sunlight the shed listed awkwardly to one side; dark, cold, full of secrets.

When the four trooped into the kitchen Ilse was leaning against the sink, her arms crossed. "*Dein freundinnen* must leave. The Colonel and *Frau* Moore coming back, *schnell.*" She glared at Peggy and Harold.

"Now, hold on a minute. Mama and Daddy wouldn't want them to leave without a snack; they're company." Joan looked at Kiki for confirmation.

"That's right," Kiki muttered, shaking off thoughts of the ghostly child. "Their father is Daddy's *freund.* You sure you want to kick them out, Ilse?"

"*Ach du lieber gott!*" With a last, evil glare, Ilse strode from the kitchen.

"I see what you mean." Peggy pulled a chair out from the table and sat. "She's a witch."

"Yeah. Probably lives in the Black Forest." Harold perched awkwardly next to his sister. "You don't actually have to give us food." He grinned. "Unless you want to."

Peggy ignored him and leaned toward Joan. "I agree that we should get permission from your dad before we go in the shed." She gave an involuntary shiver. "There's something strange about it."

Joan, startled. glanced at Kiki. "You're the one who usually 'feels' things. What do you think? Should we ask Daddy?"

Kiki, leaning against the door and looking out through the glass panel, pulled her thoughts back to the kitchen. "If it was just us, it would be *verboten*; Daddy's way to busy. You're guests, though. He won't say *Nein* to you."

WOOF! WOOF! Roland's deep bark came from the living room.

"They're back! Good timing; let's ask him right now." Joan hurried to the front door.

Harold and Peggy stood—not quite at attention, but close—listening to Ilse's imperious, *"Guten Aben, Herr* Colonel,*"* and Daddy's greeting to Roland. When Mama pushed past Ilse and saw their two young visitors, her face lit up in a smile.

"Well, hello! You're General Brown's children, aren't you? I met your mother the other day. I must say, there's quite a family resemblance." Mama glanced at Joan. "I hope your new friends can stay for dinner."

"Oh, no thank you." Peggy spoke up, flustered. "We just came over to explore the back yard." She looked across the kitchen to Daddy. "Joan and Kiki said you might want to supervise when we look in the shed, sir. Just in case."

Kiki crossed her fingers behind her back. *Say yes, Daddy. Please!*

Daddy finished hanging his coat and hat on the hall tree before he spoke.

"We can give it a quick walk-through. I've been meaning to check it out, anyway." As he reached for his leather flight jacket, he saw Harold still standing at attention. "At ease, soldier," he said, smiling. Kiki exhaled.

"Yes, sir!" Harold shifted his weight and leaned against the doorway, grinning.

While everyone milled around putting on coats, locating a flashlight and explaining that they'd gotten the shed door open, "Just for a minute, to let out the stale air," Kiki sidled up to Daddy and put a tentative hand on his arm. He looked down at the mittened hand, then into her eyes.

"What's up, Squirt?" It came out whispered, soft.

He hadn't called her that pet name in years; hearing it almost made her forget what she needed to say. "There's something you need to know, Daddy."

He put his head closer to hers. "What?"

"Remember the girl in Napa that told you where I was when Harry kidnapped me?"

The smile left Daddy's face. He looked quickly at the family and friends moving around the kitchen, then leaned in close to Kiki. "Yeah, so?"

"The shed's got one. A little boy." It took every ounce of courage for Kiki to speak. This subject was *verboten*--the sixth sense Col. Moore and his youngest daughter shared had long been a source of shame and ridicule for him--and she knew he wouldn't be happy to learn about a ghost at their new home.

Daddy straightened, rubbing his chin. Then he nodded, murmuring, "Stay close to me," and opened the kitchen door. "Let's go, troops. The day's not getting any younger."

When the five of them stepped out into the back yard's shadowy, twenty-degree air, Joan led the way, chattering nervously: "Is that your lock, Daddy? We had to take the whole thing off to get in. We didn't break it, did we?"

"At ease, Joan. I would've done the same thing. That lock's probably older than you are. God knows where the key is."

"Do you think it was used as a bomb shelter, sir?" Peggy had evidently picked up on Joan's nervousness, because she looked anxiously around.

The yard was small. A stretch of grass—now snow-covered —was flanked on one side by a clothesline, on the other by a dismal-looking vegetable patch. The windowless, age-blackened wooden building referred to as a shed stood against a stone wall at the rear of the property.

"More than likely. We'll soon find out." Colonel Brown pulled the shed door open and leaned in. "Looks like a lot of nothing in here." His voice had an echo.

"*Ich bin* first to go in." Ilse had followed them from the house. She stood behind the others, her face shadowed in the twilight.

"Ilse? *Warum bist du guer drauban?*" Why are you out here? "Go back inside." Colonel Moore's tone was curt.

Ilse opened her mouth, then clamped it shut and hurried back up the steps. Kiki and the others glanced from Daddy to the *fraulien*. Joan suppressed a grin. Everyone followed the beam of the colonel's flashlight into the shed.

They stepped into a small room, empty except for an open crate turned on its side. They saw no lawn mower, no gardening tools, not even the odd broken lamp or chair.

Kiki huddled in the crook of Daddy's arm, her eyes closed. When she realized she felt nothing out of the ordinary in the stuffy air, she opened one eye. Seeing only cobwebbed corners and a stone floor, she relaxed her grip on her father's sleeve.

"Creepy place." The colonel's voice was quiet. "Not much to investigate." He glanced at his younger daughter. "Been closed up a long time." He stepped away from Kiki and circled the room, tapping walls and running his finger along cracks.

Peggy pushed against the crate. It didn't budge.

"You're a weakling, Sis. An infant could move that." Harold gave the crate a shove. It didn't move.

"Maybe it's nailed to the floor." Joan sounded bored. "There's no jewelry in here. I vote we go back in the house and get warm."

"Jewelry?" Daddy looked at Joan, eyebrows raised.

After a moment of nervous silence Harold dug in the pocket of his jeans and pulled out the tiny gold Menorah. "Your girls found this here the other day, sir. I was going to show it to my mom." He glanced at Peggy. She shook her head and turned away.

Daddy shifted his gaze to Kiki. "You found that in here?"

"It was stuck in the wood by the door, Daddy. We were going to tell you." Kiki hoped she didn't look as guilty as she felt.

"Interesting." Daddy rubbed his chin, looking somberly at his youngest daughter. "Might have belonged to the people who lived here before us."

"Uh, Colonel, sir?" Harold was on his hands and knees, peering into the open side of the crate. "You want me to push this against the wall?"

Before Daddy could answer, a deep baritone voice called from the kitchen porch. "Colonel Bill Moore? You out here with my kids?"

"In here, Pops!" Peggy opened the shed door and looked out at the handsome grey-haired officer leaning over the porch banister.

"Let's wrap this up for now. I'll take another look at that crate tomorrow." Daddy looked relieved as Peggy, Harold, then Joan hurried from the shed. When he ushered Kiki out, an arm around her shoulder, he took a final look back and froze.

Kiki froze, too. *Oh, no.* Daddy pushed her forward and slammed the shed door. He swung Kiki off her feet, tucked her under his arm, and made a dash for the kitchen steps. As they stepped inside he whispered, almost inaudibly, "Kid's in there, all right. Stay the Hell out of there, Squirt. That's an order."

"*Herr* Colonel," Ilse stepped up to them, her face flushed and angry. "*Ich muss mit der sprechen.*" I must speak with you.

The colonel glanced at his wife and turned away from both women. "Looks like that pathetic excuse for a school is good for something, Hal. Our kids have become friends. Can I offer you a cognac before you head home?"

General Brown glanced at Mama and grinned. "Not tonight, Bill. I'll take a raincheck, though. It's not easy to say No to a good cognac."

Daddy crossed the room and put an arm around his wife. "Well put, Hal. I'll expect you to cash in that raincheck soon." With Kiki and Joan trailing behind, he walked the Browns to the front door.

"Sorry we didn't find anything in the shed." Kiki muttered. "I didn't really expect to. Not on the first try, anyway." Harold glanced at his sister, smiling mischievously.

"Have your mom talk to our mom." Peggy gave Joan a knowing look. "She's a pro when it comes to finding house help."

As soon as the door closed Ilse, then Mama could be heard shouting in the kitchen. "Mama yelling? That's a first!" Kiki gulped. "Does she need our help?"

Joan shrugged. "I don't know. Maybe. Do you think they're yelling about us?"

Just then Daddy's voice rang out, loud and clear: *"Sie sind nicht vearntwortlich fúr dieses haus, Ilse."* You are not in charge of this house or any part of this property. If you think that, d*u must gehen.* You need to go."

CHAPTER NINE

I can't handle this arguing. Kiki made a dash for the stairs, Joan right behind her. They collided, ending up half-crawling to the upstairs landing.

"Du gehòrst hier nicht hin. Das tue ich!" You do not belong here. I do.

Ilse strode from the kitchen and out of the house, slamming the front door so hard it rattled on its hinges.

The girls, shocked into silence, stared down at the empty foyer. Kiki became aware, gradually, of a muffled, whimpering sound coming from the kitchen. Then Daddy's voice, low and gentle: "It's okay, honey; it's okay. I'll head to HQ right now, apply for another servant. Please don't cry."

"Ilse made Mama cry?" Kiki's fear dissolved into anger. She grabbed the railing and practically threw herself down the stairs, with Joan close behind.

"Mama! Are you hurt?" Kiki stopped short in the kitchen

doorway, suddenly self-conscious. Her mother stood next to the sink, hands covering her face. Daddy's hand was on her shoulder; he looked like he'd rather be anywhere than with his sobbing wife.

"I'm okay." Mama wiped her eyes with a dishtowel. "Ilse has left, partly because of you two." Mama's tone was soft, but the words hurt.

"We'll get someone else." Daddy sounded oddly cheerful. "And you'll mind your manners with the next maid, girls, or you'll be packed off to your grandparents in Illinois." Without looking at Mama, he hurried past his daughters and outside. As the front door closed he called back, "Have them clear out Ilse's room, Emily. And Kiki, stay out of the back yard."

"Illinois? Would he really do that?" Joan's voice trembled.

"I don't know. Germany—and promotion to colonel—has changed your father." Mama glanced at the girls, then looked away.

The sound of Daddy's Jeep—a sort of put-put, growl—faded. Mama sat at the table, staring at her hands. "Go on upstairs, both of you. You heard your father. Clear out the attic."

Joan looked at Kiki, then slid into a chair and took one of Mama's hands. Kiki sidled across the linoleum and draped an arm cautiously around Mama's shoulder. *This is new, us comforting Mama. Usually, it's the other way around.* Mama leaned a cheek against Kiki's narrow chest.

"Did Ilse try to take Daddy away from us, Mama?" Kiki whispered the words and immediately regretted them. Joan glared at her; Mama winced, then glanced at Kiki.

"Your father is a grown man. His behavior is his responsibility--especially here, where people will do anything to survive in this war-torn country." Mama lay the towel on the table and faced her daughters. "His promotion, this tour of duty here? Big change from his life in Napa; where he was a Master

Sergeant training pilots and caring for his family." The ghost of a smile hovered on Mama's face. "He ... loves us. And he wants to do a good job here. Our job—yours and mine—is to let him know we appreciate him and take care of our side of the street. For you two, that means doing your best in school and keeping a civil tongue in your head with the Germans."

Mama got to her feet. "Let's go upstairs and take a look at the attic. It may just need a good sweeping and a change of sheets."

As the three of them went up the main stairs to the narrow, tunnel-like attic stairway Mama murmured, "What happened in the shed, girls? I thought Ilse was going to pass out when she saw you opening that door."

"Nothing happened, Mama." Joan sounded surprisingly cheerful. "It's just a musty old room. All we saw was a big empty box. Harold and Peggy were so disappointed; I think they expected jewels and gold and stuff."

Kiki chimed in, "Ilse acted like it was her shed, like we didn't have a right to explore it. Even Peggy and Harold noticed."

Mama nodded. Apparently, Ilse's attitude was not a surprise.

At the top of the attic stairs the door stood open. When Mama switched on the bulb hanging from the ceiling, the girls saw a twelve-by-sixteen space with faded wallpaper and exposed rafters. A colorless, almost threadbare rug covered the floor. "The master bedroom is right below us," Mama said. "That rug isn't much help in muffling footsteps."

"Eeww." Joan whispered. "This is ugly. No wonder she hated us."

A narrow, iron-framed cot took up most of one wall, with a three-legged table and hard-backed chair under the tiny window. A book lay open on the table.

"Did she actually live here? I mean, sleep? It doesn't feel

lived in." Kiki stepped over to the table and read aloud, *"M-e-i …Mein, K-a … Kampf."*

Mama turned quickly around. *"Mein Kampf?* That's the book Hitler wrote. It's all about creating a super race." She opened the book. Looking over her shoulder, Kiki saw "Ilse Grun" scrawled on the flyleaf.

"Okay, girls." Mama was suddenly all business. "Pull the sheets off the bed and bring them downstairs." She dropped the book in her apron pocket and watched while Joan and Kiki struggled with the bedcovers.

Mama led the way back downstairs, Kiki and Joan following blindly with their burden of sheets and blankets. As she pulled the door closed behind them Kiki glanced back at the attic window. The shed was clearly visible. *Ilse could watch it from up here.*

At supper, with just Kiki, Joan and Mama at the table, Mama seemed almost contented. She placed the fish croquettes, honey-glazed carrots and boiled potatoes before her daughters with a smile.

"The good news about all of this?" Mama smiled. "I don't have to stretch our rations to include another person."

Kiki took a forkful of food. "Will she come back for the book?"

"Don't talk with your mouth full, dear." Mama frowned.

"I've heard of *Mein Kampf,*" Joan swallowed a bite of croquette. "It shows Hitler's evil plans."

The food in Kiki's mouth was suddenly tasteless.

"I'm not pleased she was reading that book here." Mama gave her head a little shake as if to dismiss the subject of Ilse. "Why did the Brown children think they'd find jewelry in our shed?"

"Jewelry?" Kiki choked on a bit of carrot.

Joan laughed. "We found a charm from someone's bracelet out there, Mama. You know how kids are—Harold thought there might be more." She grinned at her sister.

"Really? A charm? Let's have a look at it." Mama held out her hand.

She doesn't believe us. Kiki ignored Mama's open hand. "Where's Roland? It's past his dinnertime."

"The charm, Kiki. Now." Mama wiggled her fingers. "Unless there isn't one, and you two made up this story to upset Ilse."

Kiki stared down at her fingernails. She'd just recently stopped biting them and they were finally beginning to grow past her cuticles. She was very proud of them. "We didn't make it up, Mama, and we didn't upset Ilse. It was the other way around. She was mean to us. She told us she hates Americans."

"Harold took the charm to show his mom," Joan put in. "It's a little gold candlestick."

Mama studied both of the girls for a second, then exhaled. "I'll sort all of this out later." She turned to Joan. "A candlestick? You mean a candelabra?"

Kiki piped up, her voice trailing off to a whisper. "Maybe. The kind with a bunch of candles on one stand. Harold called it a Menorah--it's a church thing." *Did I just break my promise not to tell about the Browns being Jewish?*

"Well. That makes sense. Your father said the people who lived here were Jewish." Mama pushed away from the table and stood. "Joan, it's your turn to wash the dishes. Kiki, your turn to dry." As she finished speaking, the front door opened and Roland galloped in. He skidded to a stop in front of Mama, tongue out in an eager grin.

"I'll feed him, Mama." Kiki left the table and went to the pantry as Colonel Moore came in on a draft of cold air. "Save some for me, Emily?"

"You didn't eat at the Club?" Mama spoke with her back to Daddy, her tone brusque.

"Ouch! Direct hit." Daddy lowered himself into a chair,

chuckling. "I found Sergeant Wright. It took a while; he starts his weekend early at the Club. Lucky stiff's single." The words were slightly slurred and his breath smelled like cognac. "He'll send a new *fraulein* round in a couple o' days." After swallowing a forkful of fish croquette, he looked around. "Where's Kiki?"

"Here." Kiki left the pantry and put a dish of kibble under Roland's nose. "Did you tell him to get us someone who likes Americans, Daddy?"

At Kiki's words, Mama glared first at Kiki, then at Daddy. *Oh, boy. Shouldn't have said that.* Kiki ducked her head, wishing she was invisible.

"Girls, get the dishes done. It's almost your bedtime." Mama's tone, a mix of anger and sadness, was one Kiki had seldom heard. Daddy looked from Kiki to Mama, then shook his head and bent over his half-finished supper.

Half an hour later the girls sat on the upstairs landing, listening to the rise and fall of Daddy's baritone and Mama's wispy alto. With the kitchen door closed, the words were muffled.

"Is this my fault, Joan? Did Ilse lose her temper because I wanted to explore the shed?" A feeling of dread settled over Kiki. *What if Daddy leaves us? What if he sends us back to the States? That would break Mama's heart.* She hugged her shoulders, willing herself to let go of the dark thoughts.

"What? Of course not. Nobody pays any attention to you. You're the baby, for crying out loud." Joan's voice, tentative and shaky, didn't match her words. "Daddy's been hanging out too much at the Officers' Club. When we were in Napa he wasn't an officer, so he came home on time every night."

The voices in the kitchen stopped. The girls heard Mama's

light tread on the linoleum, then saw a strip of light as the door opened and Roland pushed through. He bounded up the stairs, giving each girl a slobbery greeting kiss.

After giggling, cuddling him and wiping their cheeks, the girls went into their bedroom, Roland with them.

"I wonder where that charm came from, really." Joan looked idly out the window onto the dark street below. "And, how did it come off its' bracelet? Was it ripped off when some girl was attacked by Nazis?" She turned and frowned at Kiki.

Kiki stopped rubbing Roland's ears and stared at her. "What I wonder," she mused, "is why Ilse got so upset when we went in the shed. What's the big deal?"

"Maybe it was her charm." Joan's eyes widened. "I never thought of that."

"Not unless she's Jewish." Kiki shook her head. "Maybe she knows more about the house than she lets on."

"If only we knew what happened to the people before us. Were they victims of the Nazis? Were they kicked out by the Allies?" Joan picked up her pencil and began doodling in the margin of her notebook.

Should I tell her about the little boy ghost? No. She already thinks I'm crazy.

Kiki slipped on her shoes and began tying them. Roland, stretched out near the door, turned his head slightly and cocked one ear.

"Now, where are you going?" Joan sounded tired. "Outside? You're afraid of the dark, remember? And, the Parents will see you. We don't need to be any more in trouble."

Kiki turned, her hand on the doorknob. "It will keep me from thinking about losing Daddy." She gulped. "I'll take Roland with me. Can I borrow your flashlight?"

"C'mon, Kiki. They're just having a fight. That's what grown-ups do." Joan sighed. "You'll understand, someday. Please don't go outside. I'll have to go with you and I really,

really don't want to."

"Tell you what: If I'm not back in fifteen minutes, call the MPs" Kiki tried to smile. "I'll be fine; honest. I don't even want you to come. You'd just get in the way." She snapped on Roland's leash and slipped out of the room.

The bedroom door clicked shut, Kiki and Roland stood in the dim light of the upstairs landing listening to the murmur of voices from the kitchen. *Are they still arguing? What if Daddy was serious about sending us back to the States?*

Kiki knelt, put her finger to her lips to shush Roland, and crept silently down the stairs. When her foot touched the bottom step she stopped, peering around the railing. Staticky music could be heard from the kitchen. *They're listening to the radio. Maybe they're through fighting.* She crept to the front door and opened it just enough to slip through, then stepped out onto the porch with Roland.

Nighttime, beyond the warmth and security of the house, felt like enemy territory. Sweat trickled from Kiki's scalp in spite of the bitter cold. She clicked on Joan's flashlight, saw and felt Roland's thick fur next to her leg, and took a calming breath. *I can do this. I have to, for whoever owned that Menorah and for the child who died in our shed.*

Moving stealthily—Kiki told herself she was invisible in the dark—she and Roland made their way across patches of snow and dead grass to a back corner of the house. Noting how easily the dog fell into step with her, Kiki figured he'd been a sentry dog during the war. *"Braver Junge."* Good boy.

Because the Moores lived at the end of *Vierstrausse,* with empty houses across the lane and next to them, the front and side yard was dense black. The back, though, was dimly lit by light from the kitchen window.

As they stepped onto the path to the shed Roland suddenly stopped, pressing against Kiki so she had to stop, too. "What's up?" She squinted into the shadows. *Do I turn on the flashlight?*

No. Mama and Daddy would see it.

As her eyes adjusted, Kiki could make out someone almost as tall as her father at the shed door. The figure stepped back, pulling the door open. For a split second the kitchen window's light illuminated a *babushka*—scarf—not quite covering a knot of blonde hair. *Ilse.*

Roland growled, low in his throat. "Ssh," Kiki whispered. *I'll lock the door on her and get Daddy.*

Kiki stepped out of the house's shadow and crossed the yard. As she reached for the metal door handle, she felt Roland go limp. In the next instant an arm wrapped around her and something was jammed into her mouth. As she struggled, a foul-smelling cloth came down over her head.

CHAPTER TEN

"Achtung! Was ist los?"

Daddy! Kiki heard her father's shout. "Uummph!" Her own cry didn't make it past the rag jammed against her teeth.

"Ach, mein lieber gott!" Kiki's captor snarled, pushing her violently to the ground.

She lay there, stunned. She slowly became aware of a different touch, this one gentle. Then, Daddy's gravelly whisper. "Hold still, Squirt, so I can get you out of this goddammed thing."

When Colonel Moore pulled back the cloth—a burlap bag, scratchy and stinking of rotten cabbage—he lifted Kiki to her feet in a bear hug. "You okay?"

He let go of his daughter and dropped to his knees. "Goddammit! They killed my dog!"

Kiki felt herself shaking uncontrollably. "Roland! Wake up, boy. Please don't be dead." Tears rolled down her cheeks.

Daddy put a hand on the dog's head and gently stroked the patch of fur between Roland's ears. One eye opened. Roland looked up, saw Daddy and struggled to his feet.

"Thank God," Daddy muttered. His arm encircled Kiki's shivering form. "What the Hell were you doing out here this time of night? And with my dog! You could have both been killed."

"S-s-sorry, Daddy. S-s-sorry." Kiki's teeth were chattering so, she could hardly make her lips form words.

"Let's get you inside." With one hand on Roland's collar Daddy guided Kiki up the kitchen steps and into the kitchen.

"Emily!" Daddy shouted. "Emily!"

From the stairs Mama responded, "I'm coming. What's wrong?"

As soon as Mama appeared in the kitchen doorway, Daddy was out the back door. He called back, "Someone tried to kidnap Kiki. And Roland took a hit to the head."

"For heaven's sake!" Mama bustled across the kitchen to her younger daughter huddled miserably at the back door. "You were outside at night? With Roland? What possessed you to do such a thing?"

Kiki's eyes filled with new tears. "I just wanted to look in the shed. Someone grabbed me and put a bag over my head. I couldn't breathe. They hit Roland. I thought he was dead." She dropped into a chair, brought her knees up to her chin and began sobbing..

"Oh, dear." The anger left Mama's face. She wrapped her arms around Kiki. "Okay, honey. It's over now. You're safe." After a minute she murmured, "It must have felt like that terrible experience in Napa. I'm so sorry this happened." She stroked Kiki's hair, humming softly. "Down in the valley, valley so low …."

Roland had retreated to his wicker bed near the stove. Now, he got unsteadily to his feet and crossed the linoleum to lean against Kiki, his chin on her leg. As she stroked his head, the horror of the past minutes faded.

Daddy's out there in the dark, looking for the attacker. Kiki sat up. "What if they kidnap Daddy? Should we call the MPs, Mama?"

"Not just yet. Your father can take care of himself." Mama drummed her fingers on the table. "Joan said you were in the back yard. We thought she was making it up, trying to get you in trouble."

At the judgment in Mama's voice, Kiki winced. *It's my fault Daddy's out there now, in danger.*

Mama must have noticed. She murmured, "Tell me what happened, why you went out there." She sighed. "We need to figure out why there was an intruder in our yard." She looked nervously toward the back door.

Kiki straightened. "To get in the shed. That's the only reason I can think of."

Mama shook her head. "That makes no sense. Unless, maybe, they needed shelter? Not likely, though on private property."

Kiki remembered how Roland had acted when they stepped outside. like he was on sentry duty. "Roland growled, and he stayed really close to me."

"He must have known someone was out there." Mama smoothed Kiki's hair back from her forehead. "Can you remember anything about the person who grabbed you? Was it a man? I'm wondering if it was Ilse, come back to get revenge."

Kiki closed her eyes. *It was so awful. Do I have to think about it? Yes.* "The person smelled bad. Like Daddy when he's been to the Club."

"They smelled like cigarettes? Whisky?"

Kiki nodded. "And dirt. Dirt and leaves, like the forest." She quickly amended, "Daddy never smells like dirt." She attempted a smile, failed. "I think Ilse was there. I saw her hair.

But she didn't grab me. That was a man. A rough, mean *herr*."

"Did you hear their voices?"

Kiki paused, frustrated at the blank spot in her memory, "I heard something like, '*Schnapp dir das maddchen.*' It came from across the yard." She stared at Mama. "What does that mean?"

Mama rubbed her eyes. She looked tired. "*Maddchen* means girl. The rest? I'm not sure."

At that moment the kitchen doorknob turned; Mama froze. Kiki emitted a tiny shriek. Daddy stepped in, rubbing his hands together and shivering.

"No luck. The *schweinehund's* long gone." He went to the table, running a gentle hand along Kiki's shoulder, and lowered his shivering bulk into a chair. "Damn, it's cold out there!"

Joan appeared in the kitchen doorway. "What's going on? What have I missed?" She glanced at Kiki. "I told her not to go out."

Mama shook her head almost imperceptibly. She gently moved Kiki off her lap and went to the stove. "Do you want tea, Bill, or would a cognac warm your insides better?"

"Tea, Emily. Much as I'd prefer a cognac, I need to stay focused." Daddy leveled his gaze at his younger daughter. "Like I told you when you got here, the war is over, but this is still a war zone. Some of the Germans still consider us the enemy. I'd like to report this to the authorities—the MPs," he glanced at Mama, "but the most they'd do is write a report." He looked at Joan hovering in the doorway. "Take a seat, sister. Both of you, listen closely." He glanced from Kiki to Joan. "Tomorrow morning, bright and early, we do a thorough investigation of the shed. I want to know what's in there," he avoided looking at Kiki, "that's worth stealing." Until then—the rest of this night— you are both confined to quarters. *Verstehst?*"

"But, Daddy, what about the …?" Kiki's voice trailed off. *I guess the ghost child isn't worth stealing.*

Mama cut in, "Kiki, anything in the shed now will be there in the morning. As your father said, the outdoors at night is not safe for you."

Joan had been quiet while the conversation swirled around her. Now, she snapped, "Will someone please tell me what's going on? I told her not to go out there!"

Daddy stared at his older daughter. "You knew she was going outside? Why the hell didn't you stop her? She's just a kid; you're old enough to know better."

Joan's mouth snapped shut. She folded her arms, looking down at the table. Mama looked surprised, but she said nothing. Kiki blurted, "She tried to stop me. I thought you wouldn't notice because you were arguing about Ilse."

The kitchen was completely silent for a second. Then a small, *pffft* from Roland's hindquarters broke the spell. Mama looked at Daddy, whose face had gone from red to pasty white. "It's time we started acting like a family again, Bill. All of us. If there's anything positive to take from," her voice dropped to a whisper, "the encounter with Ilse, it's that wake-up call. We haven't been functioning as a team here. This attack in our back yard brings that weakness front and center."

Colonel Moore looked down at his hands. "You're right, Emily. As usual. In my defense, Napa seemed a lifetime away, you there and me here. You were doing a great job, running things without me. I counted on that even after you got here." He looked up at his wife, tears glistening in the corners of his eyes.

Daddy's crying! Oh, no! Is it my fault?

Emily Moore did not look at her husband. Instead, she turned to Joan. "Kiki and Roland were attacked when they went out to the shed. Your father scared off the attacker, but he got away. We don't know if Ilse was part of the attack, but we're suspicious." She finished with a tiny smile. "You are not responsible for your sister's behavior. With everything that's been going on around here, it's understandable you wouldn't want to bother us."

Joan and Kiki both stared, openmouthed. An apology by either of their parents? Kiki didn't know it was possible. Joan recovered first. She touched Kiki's hand, smiling sweetly. "You poor thing! You were attacked again? You must be cursed!"

Kiki struggled to suppress an urge to smack the smile off Joan's face. "Right," she muttered.

"Before you go back to bed," Colonel Moore cleared his throat. "what's your take on the shed, Joan? Any idea why someone wants to get in there?"

Joan sat back, looking pleased at being addressed as an equal. "Well, let's see: We did find some jewelry in there. Not much, but still …. and that crate. What's it doing, sitting there empty like that? Oh, hold on!" Her face lit up. "Daddy, didn't Harold say it had hinges? Is that normal?"

"My goodness," Mama broke in, "the ideas get wilder and wilder. Time for bed, everyone." She stood and began clearing the table.

"Hit the sack, girls. And this time, Kiki, stay there. That's an order." Daddy's voice was gruff, but not harsh. On an impulse, Kiki ran to him and gave him a hug. "Thanks for saving me, Daddy," she whispered.

"Always, Squirt," he whispered into her hair.

Getting into pajamas and brushing her teeth, Kiki carefully ignored Joan. *Maybe the parents aren't mad at her, but I am. She thinks she's so much better than me, just because she was born first. I wish my sixth sense was catching, like cooties. I'd rub it all over her.*

When the lights were out and the girls lay hugging either edge of the bed, Kiki heard Joan murmur, "God, please bless my sister and do a better job of protecting her. I don't know what I'd do if something happened to her."

Remorse immediately flooded Kiki. Her own bedtime prayer had been short; anger and humility didn't mix. Now she rolled over on her back, hands together. "One more thing, God. Thanks for sending Daddy outside tonight. He saved my life. Also, keep an eye on Roland, will you? He's a war veteran; he doesn't need more stress."

"Night, Kiki," came quietly from Joan's side of the bed.

"Night, Joan." Kiki exhaled. *I'm not a bit sleepy. I wish I could* ….

Hours later, sound asleep and dreaming about empty, abandoned houses full of cobwebs, Kiki sat up in bed. "What did you say?" Her own voice woke her. *Is Joan talking in her sleep?*

The room was not completely dark, even in the wee hours of the morning; Germany was too close to the North Pole for that. Kiki peered into the dimness of three a.m., trying to recall the words that had pulled her out of a sound sleep. Other than her sister's even, slightly nasal breathing, all was silent. The mirror across the room reflected, darkly, the image of a big-eyed, messy-haired girl sitting up in bed and looking around. *I guess I was dreaming.* Kiki twitched in an involuntary shiver and eased back down onto the pillow, then lifted her head for a last look across the room.

The rocking chair in the corner by the window—Joan's favorite place to sit and do homework—moved. As Kiki watched, it began rocking back and forth. *Is the wind doing that? Did we leave the window open? No. the window's shut tight. Is there an earthquake, like in California? Nothing else is moving, so, no.*

She became aware of soft, almost indiscernible humming. As she strained to listen, the tune from one of Daddy's German drinking songs became clear: 'Ach, du liebe Augustine,

Augustine, Augustine ...' blended with the back and forth of the rocking chair.

Slowly, silently, Kiki crept from the bed, wincing when her bare feet touched the cold floor. Wrapping her arms around herself against the chill, she glided across the room and stopped a foot from the rocker. As it moved back and forth, up and down, an idea surfaced. *When Joan rocks, the floor creaks. It's not creaking now.* "I know that song," she whispered.

The humming stopped. The rocking stopped. *"Du bist eine Deutsch fraulein?"* a high, small-child voice broke the room's silence.

"No. *Nein.* American," Kiki felt herself become very still, very focused. "Are you Jewish?"

"Nicht verstehen." I don't understand. *"Wo ist mutter?"* Where is mama?

CHAPTER ELEVEN

Am I dreaming? Kiki stood still, taking a mental inventory. *I don't think so. Maybe. Might as well just go with it.* "Are you the little boy from the shed?" As her eyes adjusted to the dim light she saw the form of the child ghost curled up in the rocking chair.

His response to her question was a blank stare. He shrugged and turned his head, rocking faster.

Kiki tried again. *"Uh, du bist der junge im schuppen?"* *I hope shuppen means shed.*

The child stopped rocking. He looked at her, fear in his small, pale face. *"Kommen die bosen manner zunuck?"* Are the bad men coming back?

What is he saying? It sounds important. "I'm sorry. I don't speak much German. Er, *Lied. No Deutch.* Did you say something about bad men? You mean, *Nazis?*"

The word '*Nazis*' resounded in the air. The child threw

himself at Kiki, pushing her to the floor.

Stunned by the force of contact with a presence which should have been little more than a puff of air, Kiki fell back against the bedpost. "Oof! Hey, no fair!" Her entire arm tingled and felt icy cold. When no more blows came, she looked around. He was gone.

On the bed above her, Joan muttered, "Tryin' to sleep here." The bedsprings creaked as the older girl turned over.

Kiki stood, rubbed her sore shoulder and looked around the room. The eerie tension of a minute ago gave way to the calm of very early morning. *Did I really talk to the ghost boy? Was it just a bad dream?*

A glance at the rocking chair—still moving, but slower—said otherwise. Kiki scrambled back to bed to lay there, terrified. Gradually Joan's nasal breathing calmed her. Putting her hands together under the covers, Kiki prayed. "God, please keep me safe. And please send an angel to rescue that little boy. You know I can't help him; I'm just a kid, myself."

"Were you up in the middle of the night?" Joan applied lipstick and looked at Kiki's reflection in the bathroom mirror.

"No! Why would I be?" The smoothness of the lie surprised Kiki. "Uh," she amended, "What makes you ask? Did you have a nightmare?"

Joan shook her head. "Something woke me—you were whispering in your sleep. You do that, you know." She fluffed her shining curls and hurried from the bathroom.

Kiki splashed her face with cold water and fluffed her own, still frizzy perm. *Daddy promised to explore the shed this morning. I hope he remembers.*

"Joan? Is everything okay with Mama and Daddy now? With Ilse gone, I mean? Do you think they'll still split up?"

Kiki's voice trembled.

The older girl turned with one hand on the stair rail. She looked at Kiki through puffy, bloodshot eyes. "I have no idea." She reached out and gave her sister a half-hug. "Be extra nice to Mama, okay?" She blew out a breath. "I don't think I ever want to get married when I grow up."

"Girls?" Mama stood at the bottom of the stairs, a pot of oatmeal in her hand.

"Morning!" Kiki took the stairs two at a time and wrapped her arms around Mama. "I love you!" she squeaked.

Mama turned back to the kitchen, chuckling. "Goodness, what brought that on?"

Joan slid into a chair at the table and poured milk on the oatmeal waiting for her, then peered into the pitcher. "This milk looks kind of creamy. Is it the real thing, Mama? Not that awful powdered stuff?" She dipped a spoon into the hot cereal.

"Are you kidding? Where would the commissary get real milk?" Kiki giggled, relieved at the morning's normalcy. Without warning, she thought of the ghost's high-pitched, wavery voice. She looked down at the creamy, brown sugar-sprinkled cereal before her. *I wonder if he liked oatmeal--when he was alive?*

"Daydreaming again, Kiki? Finish your breakfast. We have a busy day ahead of us." The smile on Mama's face didn't match her words.

"Are we still going to the Rhine River? Is it safe there?" Kiki hoped she didn't sound like a baby.

"*Ach, du Lieber Gott!* What a scaredy cat! I want to see the castles everyone talks about." Joan set her now-empty bowl in the sink. Then, in a quieter voice, "You want me to wash these, Mama?" She glared at Kiki behind Mama's back.

Emily Moore shook her head, her mouth in the firm line which meant she was thinking. "When he gets back from gassing up the Jeep, your father will take another look out back.

Be ready to go, girls. You know he hates to be kept waiting."
She smoothed Kiki's hair. "Put last night's experience behind
you. And remember, don't go out alone after dark."

I wish it was that easy. The ominously silent interior of the
shed suddenly flashed before Kiki's eyes; her stomach did a
flip-flop and she gagged, spitting out a spoonful of oatmeal. She
put down her spoon. "S-S-Sorry, Mama. Can't eat any more."
The expected criticism—gagging at the table was very bad
manners—didn't come. Without a word Mama picked up Kiki's
oatmeal bowl.

"But," Joan blurted, "she's wasting food. She can't get away
with that!"

Mama stopped half-way to the sink, frowning. "What did
you say, young lady?"

Brraap! The Jeep's horn sounded from the driveway.

"Daddy's back!" Kiki practically threw herself off the chair
and ran from the kitchen. "I'll meet him out front."

"Doesn't look so scary in the daylight, does it?" The look
Daddy gave Kiki was far kinder than usual. "Let's walk along
the fence, then do a recon of the shed."

Kiki put a timid hand on her father's sleeve. "You know
that, er, ghost we saw in the shed yesterday--the little boy? He
was in our room last night. He kicked me." Kiki held her breath,
praying Daddy was in the mood to talk about this forbidden
subject.

Daddy stopped—he'd walked away, toward the back fence
—and slowly turned to look at his youngest daughter. Whatever
he saw in her face must have convinced him she wasn't lying; he
covered the distance between them in two long strides. "It's on
the move? That's not good, Squirt." He shook his head. "Child
or not, we need to get rid of it."

The tension gripping Kiki since last night melted away. *He understands.* She held tight to her father's coat sleeve and followed him inside the shed.

Colonel Moore's Army-issued flashlight projected light from one wall to another. "Gotta be more to this place than meets the eye," he muttered. "It's too small, even for storage." He gave the crate an experimental kick with his foot. It didn't budge. "I'm thinking this covers the steps to a root cellar. Or a bomb shelter." He studied Kiki's slightly pinched, freckled face. "There's probably nothing more than a few rotten potatoes down there, Squirt. Do you have the stomach for this?" When Kiki nodded, Col. Moore knelt, wrapped his arms around the side of the crate, and lifted.

.   Kiki dropped to her knees to look beneath the crate. "You're right. There's a trapdoor, Daddy." "Want me to pull it open? There's no lock."

"Bill!" Mama's voice called from the back porch.

"What, now?" Col. Moore frowned. He lowered the crate to the floor, calling back, "In here, Emily!"

A moment later Mama's figure blocked the weak sunlight coming through the shed's doorway. "There's a Lieutenant Martin here to see you." She sounded nervous. "About Ilse, I think."

Daddy straightened, pressing one hand to his spine. "Never a dull moment. This root cellar will have to wait." He glanced at Kiki. "Get Joan. Both of you, wait for us in the Jeep." He strode across the yard and into the house without looking back. Kiki stood in the shed's doorway, blinking back tears. *We figured out what the crate was hiding. We found the cellar door. We shouldn't stop now!*

"Kiki! Inside. Now." Mama's voice was tense.

Kiki put one foot in front of the other, feeling hopeless. When she stepped into the kitchen Mama whispered, "Go straight through the living room and out the front door, quiet as a ghost. Joan's already in the Jeep. We'll be out as soon as the lieutenant leaves."

"Did we get Daddy in trouble, Mama?" Kiki whispered back. "Did Ilse tell on us?"

Mrs. Moore turned away, shaking her head. She walked quickly into the living room and stood, arms folded and frowning. next to the lieutenant.

What's going on? Isn't she on Daddy's side?

Only years of training as a military dependent got Kiki across the living room and outside without notice by the adults. As the front door clicked shut she heard the lieutenant's bass rumble: "Serious charge ... responsibility to set a good example ..."

The Jeep's side door was open. When Kiki approached, Joan stuck her head out. "Hurry! Get in!" Tears had demolished Joan's carefully-applied make-up. She looked out at Kiki through puffy eyes.

"What can we do?' Kiki climbed into the Jeep. "Will Daddy get court martialed because of us?"

Joan turned even more pale. She put up two fingers in an X. "Jinx," she hissed. "Saying so could make it happen!"

"That's crazy." Kiki recoiled. "You know I'd never wish that on Daddy. He's talked about becoming an officer, being someone important, my whole life."

"I know. I know." Tears rolled down Joan's cheeks. "It's this rotten country. No matter what we do, we're in trouble and hurting someone. I hate it here!" She punched the Jeep's metal frame, then drew back her fist. Staring wide-eyed at her sore hand, she looked pathetic. Kiki realized, for the first time. that her impossibly grown-up sister was just another kid, scared and vulnerable. "Let's make a plan. You know, like Daddy taught us: Always have an escape plan in case things go sour." She gave Joan what she hoped was an encouraging smile.

Joan's face lit up in a lopsided grin. "Right. First of all, we don't admit fault no matter what. It's that *fraulein*'s word against ours. Far as anyone knows, we're Snow White; well, I am. You're Dopey or Sneezy; take your pick."

Kiki let out the breath she'd been holding. "And Ilse, she's the wicked queen." She paused. "Do you think Daddy would really send us back to Illinois?" She answered her own question. "In a heartbeat, if it meant keeping his colonel's wings."

Joan was quiet for a full minute. Finally, she muttered, "He wouldn't want to, though. He does love us. It's just… he has trouble prioritizing. I think it's a guy thing."

Kiki turned away, trying to make sense of this grown-up logic. "What can we do to help? Maybe Daddy's rules don't apply in *Deutschland*. Maybe we should take the fall for him." She looked timidly at her sister.

Joan sat up straight. "You're a genius! C'mon! We have to go in there and tell that lieutenant everything's our fault, and that we're sorry." She stared hard at Kiki.

"Lie, you mean?" Kiki's voice shook.

"Like a rug. Like a homemade, Granny rag rug!"

As Kiki followed Joan up the steps and into the house, her head ready to explode with the seriousness of Joan's request, she hissed, "What do we say?"

"Say we want Ilse back, that we're sorry and we'll be nice to her from now on!"

Kiki flashed on Ilse's smug, superior expression. *Can I do that? What about someone trying to kidnap me? What about the little ghost?* "Are you sure this will work?" she whispered to Joan's back.

The front door opened and the lieutenant, grim and tight-lipped, stepped around them onto the porch. Kiki's glance went to Colonel Moore. He stood shadowed in the doorway.

"Wait, sir! Don't leave yet!' Kiki's voice came out in a frantic squeak.

"Yes," Joan chimed in. "Stay a minute. Please."

All three adults stared at the girls. Before Daddy or, worse, the lieutenant could silence them, Joan continued, "Please. We're sorry we made trouble for the *fraulein* and our parents. It isn't Daddy's fault, it's ours. My sister and I," she glanced at Kiki, "promise to be respectful and obedient to *frauleins*, even when they are bossy and mean to us." Joan batted her eyelashes at the lieutenant.

The lieutenant stared first at Colonel Moore, then at the girls. "You made trouble for the maid?" His gray eyes went to Kiki. "Tell me about that."

"Uh, er," Kiki squeaked, "We didn't let her help us with our homework. And we didn't tell her where we were going when we went to Harold and Peggy's house." *Dear God, is that enough? I can't tell him about the salt in the coffee. That would get us sent back to the States, for sure.*

"What's your take on this, Colonel?"

"It's news to me," Daddy muttered. I'll speak to my wife about it."

Mama appeared at the door. "I cautioned the girls about obeying Ilse when I'm away from the house." She studied her daughters' scared faces. "They have a lot to learn about conduct around servants." She paused. "As do we all."

The lieutenant nodded. "I'll leave this matter to you, ma'am." He saluted Daddy and hurried down the steps. As he drove away, he glanced at them. He looked sad.

"Stay in the car, both of you. We'll be out *mach schnell*," Daddy growled.

"What's going on?" Joan called across the yard to Mama. "Are we in trouble?"

"No." Mama shook her head, then stepped inside and closed the door.

In the Jeep a few minutes later—Colonel Moore stiff-backed and silent in the driver's seat, Mama stone-faced beside him—Daddy switched off the staticky radio. "God-damned polka music!"

Joan straightened, glancing at Kiki. "Are we being sent home?"

Daddy's eyes flicked from Joan to Mama, then straight ahead. It looked, to Kiki, like he was crying.

Mama spoke up, her voice calm. "It's complicated, girls." She paused. "I think it helped, what you told the lieutenant about ..." she choked on the next word, "Ilse."

Nothing more was said about the lieutenant's visit. The road stretched out before the olive-green Jeep as the Rhine River, a place real to Kiki only through storybooks, beckoned.

"Uh, Daddy?" Kiki's voice was hoarse from the prolonged silence. Colonel Moore's eyes, dark and flat, met hers in the rearview mirror. "Why is the river we're going to such a big deal? The one in Napa goes right through the town and ends up in the bay, but we don't brag about it."

Colonel Moore took the cigar out of his mouth and held it between two fingers. "You'll see. The Napa River is not much more than a mud puddle compared to the Rhine."

"Bigger? It's bigger?"

He nodded. "Bigger, longer, deeper. So big, it has islands in the middle with castles on them." His tone lifted as he spoke. Mama looked back at Kiki and smiled.

CHAPTER TWELVE

The drive from Bad Kissingen to the banks of the Rhine--
three hours on metal seats in the open-air vehicle -- took the
Moore family along the outskirts of the Black Forest. They
drove through hills covered in grey, frozen potato plants, past
weedy orchards of dead-looking fruit trees, and through tiny
villages Mama called, 'hamlets.' The second time she used that
word, Joan giggled, "I thought Hamlet was a guy in an old
play."

Daddy chuckled, then glanced at Mama and frowned. She
wasn't talking to him, and certainly wasn't in the mood for
humor.

Kiki, also not in the mood for jokes, passed the time looking
for Nazi swastikas. She saw, instead, American flags fluttering
ostentatiously from balconies in all of the tiny villages. *They
want us to know they're glad we're here. And maybe they don't
want us to hurt them.*

The atmosphere in the Jeep remained cool. Mama looked straight ahead; Daddy chewed on his cigar and fiddled with the radio. At finding only polkas played by tinny-sounding accordions he muttered, "Why the hell can't they play a little Benny Goodman?" He switched the radio off.

Mama sighed. She glanced at Daddy. "Let's put this behind us, Bill. We're still a family. That's what counts. Lord knows, I'm as ignorant as anyone when it comes to dealing with house-help."

Daddy gave a curt nod, saying nothing.

Did he hear her? Why didn't he answer? Kiki glanced at Joan. Her sister looked back, rolling her eyes in an "I have no idea," gesture.

"Uh, Daddy?" Kiki tried to sound casual, didn't quite make it.

Daddy's eyes, curiously expressionless, met hers in the rearview mirror.

"The Napa River goes through Napa. Is this river named after a town?"

Daddy removed the cigar from his mouth and dropped it in the ashtray. "I don't think so. It starts in the Alps, in Switzerland. The part that goes through Germany? It makes the Napa River look like the creek on our property back home. The Rhine has played a key part in German history."

Kiki was quiet a minute, appreciating this rare expansiveness from her father. "History? Like, the war?"

"Yep. Other wars, too, going back to medieval times. The castles you'll see today? They were built on those islands for protection from invaders." Daddy exhaled noisily. "We're almost there."

Mama had been still so long, sitting erect and staring out the windshield, Kiki was startled when she turned her head and gave her younger daughter the shadow of a smile.

Joan immediately piped up, "I can't wait! I'm sure **I'll** like the Rhine lots more than the old Napa River." She gave Kiki a triumphant, sidelong glance.

Kiki sat back against the metal seat and stared unseeing at the side flaps. *This trip would be fun if Joan wasn't here making me look bad. Why wasn't I an only child? Then, maybe, Mama and Daddy would appreciate me.* She huddled on the edge of the seat, feeling guilty, defensive and a little scared.

"Mama, Kiki's pouting again." Joan glanced at her sister. "Must you always be such a baby? Can't you see Mama and Daddy are trying to do something nice for us?"

"That's enough, Joan," Daddy growled. Kiki straightened and ran a sleeve along her face. "Sorry, Daddy. Sorry, Mama."

Neither parent turned to look at her. *Did they hear me?* Just then Colonel Moore's hand left the steering wheel and reached into the back of the Jeep. He gripped Kiki's knee and gave it a squeeze.

Kiki turned so her back was to Joan and peered out through a crack in the side flap. *I'll pretend she's not here.* As her eyes refocused, she caught sight of a cylindrical stone tower standing abandoned against the blue-white sky. Grey and weathered, it looked ancient. *Was that made by God Himself?* Kiki smiled. Her hand came up and she waved at it.

The Jeep rounded a curve in the road, leaving the tower behind. Another stone structure appeared, so close to the road Kiki could have reached out and touched it. She looked up along the rough grey wall to a cross perched high above. *This one's a church.* Weeds grew on all sides, obscuring all but a bit of blackened wood at a door. A tree branch reached out through a glassless window.

No one cares about that church, or about the tower. That is so sad. She turned away, looking out the front windshield as the Jeep rounded a curve. There, directly before them, was a wide expanse of sparkling, gray-blue water.

"Oh, my," Mama whispered.

"Like I said. Big." Daddy's voice was soft.

He was right. The Rhine was wider than any river Kiki had ever seen. Looking from left to right, water stretched to the horizon. Straight ahead, a mountain sloped to the river's far bank. And, yes, islands with round, peaked-roof stone towers could be seen up and downstream.

"Castles! Look! Fairytale castles!" Kiki and Joan both squealed.

"We'll head through those trees for a better look." Daddy pulled the Jeep to a stop and climbed out. He took a breath, shuddered, and gave Kiki a quick glance. Then, seeming to shake off some first impression, he said, "A lot has happened along these banks. Notice this trampled ground, girls? And, that's Switzerland across the river."

Kiki, Joan and Mama got out and looked far across the river to a tree-covered mountainside dotted with colorful, happy-looking buildings. "Very pretty." Joan sounded a little bored.

Kiki looked, but her thoughts were on Daddy's comment about the trampled grass. "Was it trampled by people, Daddy? People trying to get out of Germany?" She sensed fear ranging on terror in the air around them. *Oh, boy.* She grabbed her father's hand and held on tight.

"No, but you're close." Daddy looked down at her, his face grave. "This river is one border the Nazis couldn't protect. The Allies came in through here We took out a lot of prisoners this way."

Joan shrugged, walking ahead through the trees.

Kiki tried to shake off the aura of fear all around them. She concentrated on the gigantic, calmly flowing Rhine, looking downstream to another island castle. She stared at it, counting the turrets, pointed roofs, and ancient stone walls. Then, slightly less fearful, she ran to catch up with her family.

"For such an immense river it certainly is quiet." Mama stood a few yards back from the water as it lapped at ragged weeds. "It wasn't like this before the war, was it, Bill?" She stretched out her arms in a sort of river embrace. "In old pictures there were cruise ships, sailboats, yachts everywhere up and down the Rhine."

"The war took care of that." Daddy looked around. "Let's sit there and eat our lunch." He indicated a bench a few yards from the water. As Mama dug into her picnic basket he muttered, "Thanks to Lieutenant Martin, I've got to cut this trip short."

Mama looked at the girls—Joan and Kiki were perched together on one end of the bench, unwrapping brown-bread and cheese—and frowned. "We'll be back there soon enough. Concentrate on your family, Bill. God knows we get little enough of your attention."

Joan's head snapped up. Kiki stared, then looked quickly away. *Mama must be really mad; she never talks to Daddy like that.*

Colonel Moore's lip curled in a sneer. He opened his mouth to speak, then snapped it shut and turned away from the bench. He dug in his pocket for a cigar and stared across the river.

Mama took an apple from the basket. "This is a lovely spot." She sounded cheerful, but her eyes were moist.

The tension between her parents had a curious effect on Kiki. Without thinking she stood, jammed her hands in her coat pockets, and walked back along the river path toward the parking area.

After five minutes of striding angrily along, the seeping, persistent cold reminded her where she was. She looked around. The river a few feet away felt foreign, menacing. She listened, hoping to hear Joan or Mama calling her. Except for the lap, lap of water against the shore, all was completely silent.

Suddenly, jarringly, a twig snapped nearby.

"Mama? Joan?" Kiki whispered. No answer. *Stay calm. Turn around and walk back the way you came.*

She stood still, aware of the cold coming through her coat.

When a tiny, almost imperceptible scratching came from the river bank, she turned her head. Two tiny mice dashed out of the mud at her feet and into a pile of leaves. "Eek!" Kiki shuddered, then turned and stumbled back along the path.

Kiki heard Joan before she saw her. "There you are!" The older girl came into sight lugging the picnic basket.

"I bet you thought you'd get out of pack mule duty. Well, you thought wrong." Joan thrust the basket at Kiki and hurried on along the path.

"Wait! Is the picnic over? Am I in trouble?"

Mama and Daddy appeared around a curve in the path, walking stiffly and not touching. Mama must have noticed Kiki because she stopped, touching Daddy's arm. They both frowned. "Picnic's over. Hightail it to the Jeep." Daddy's voice was gruffer than usual.

Kiki did as she was told. She turned around, hoisted the picnic basket on her shoulder, and hurried back along the path. *I wish I could carry things on my head like African ladies.*

As she came into the parking area she saw Joan leaning gracefully against the Jeep and looking into her compact mirror. *She's checking her face NOW?* A family with two teen-aged boys climbed from a vehicle across the parking area. *Oh.* Kiki stowed the picnic basket in the rear of the Jeep. Joan sidled over. "Want some help, little sister?" She smiled across the lot at the boys.

"Good timing. It's all done." Kiki hoped the boys heard her.

The first part of the ride home was silent. Kiki stared out the side, trying not to think about the mice. Trouble was, those mice were the only thing keeping her thoughts away from Mama's harsh words. *Is Daddy going to send us home? I'd like that, except I want him to come with us.* She felt a sharp pain in the region of her heart. *Please let them make up, God. Please. And could you please send us all home? This place isn't good for any of us. Especially me.*

She closed her eyes. When Daddy said something about the shed, she opened them. "Can we finish looking in there when we get back, Daddy?"

Colonel Moore's intense black eyes glanced in the rearview mirror. "Not today."

Mama said, without looking at the girls, "When we get home, go straight to your room. And stay there." Her voice caught on the last word.

Colonel Moore, grim-faced, picked up the soggy stub of his cigar and stuck it between his teeth.

"Uh, Daddy?" Kiki dreaded getting between her arguing parents, but she dreaded even more another encounter with the angry little ghost. "We still have to, uh, clean out that root cellar, or whatever it is."

"That'll have to wait." Daddy tapped the steering wheel and muttered, "I have more important things to take care of."

"We'll go right to our room. We want the mess with Ilse straightened out as much as you do." Joan sounded nervous. "You deserve a nice maid, Mama. I know Daddy agrees with that. And Kiki deserves to be safe in our back yard. You can take care of all that, can't you, Daddy?" She sat back, frowning.

Wow. Who told Joan she could talk to them like that? Kiki stared at her sister.

Colonel Moore didn't react, but his wife's eyebrows went up almost to her hairline. After a second, she breathed out, "Thank you, Joan."

When he pulled into the driveway, Daddy spoke quietly into the Jeep's frosty silence. "Go on inside, Emily. I'm going to the

Club to talk to the General. I'll be damned if I'll let that *fraulein* sabotage my career."

Mama nodded and climbed from the Jeep. Kiki and Joan joined her, cringing at the awful **SCREETCH**! as Colonel Moore ground the Jeep's gears and drove away.

CHAPTER THIRTEEN

WOOF! WOOF! Roland barked furiously from an upstairs window.

"Hey, boy! How'd you get out of the kitchen?" Kiki, Mama and Joan all stared up at him.

"I hope he hasn't made a mess." Mama rounded on Kiki. "You must have left the kitchen door open."

"I didn't; I remember." Kiki hurried into the house, Joan and Mama close behind. The big dog bounded down the stairs and lunged at Kiki, licking her face ecstatically. "Whoa, Roland!"

"Sit!" Joan shouted.

Roland stopped, his paws on Kiki's shoulders, and cocked his head at Joan. After a moment's hesitation, he sat.

"Good. Now stay, Roland. Kiki, see what damage he's done upstairs. Joan, put him in the back yard." Mama sounded tired.

Tap, Tap!

Everyone looked at the front door.

Tap, Tap!

Mama got a grip on Roland's collar, then nodded to Joan to get the door. When it creaked open Ilse stood there, her shabby wool coat and head scarf covered in snow.

Mama opened the door wider. "*Guten tag*, Ilse. How can we help you?"

"*Guten tag, Frau* Moore." Ilse glanced at the girls. "*Ich bin* commanded to make peace *mit du*."

"Commanded? Really?" Mama drew herself to her full height and looked up at the younger woman.

Joan and Kiki closed their gaping mouths. As Joan slipped a protective arm around her mother's waist, Kiki hissed, "Should we sic Roland on her?"

Mama shook her head. She stepped back from the door, giving Ilse the smallest of smiles. "Please come in. *Willkommen*. It's too cold to talk--er, *sprechen*--on the porch."

As Ilse stepped inside Kiki burst out, "Were you here before we got home? Is that why Roland broke out of the kitchen? You were at our front door?"

Ilse looked puzzled, but nodded. "*Ja, vol.*" The face she turned to Mrs. Moore was devoid of its usual haughty expression. She looked uncomfortable. Unhappy.

"Girls, go in the kitchen and put the kettle on. Stay there until I call you." Mama stared at Joan and Kiki until they sidled from the living room, glowering at Ilse.

Just inside the kitchen door, Joan turned. "Was it you who grabbed Kiki last night, Ilse?"

Mama and Kiki looked first to Joan, then to Ilse. The *fraulein's* face paled. "*Gott in Himmel, No!*" She stared at Kiki. "*Bist du verletzt?* Are you hurt?"

"An intruder came onto our property and attacked her last night." Mama's words were clipped. "The girls thought it was you. They knew how angry you were."

"*Mein Gott, liebschen!* I had nothing to do with that. Believe me, *bitte*. My *werargerung*---my anger—not to *kinder*." Her shoulders drooped. She looked almost pathetic.

"I believe you. Please have a seat. Who did you say commanded you to come here?" Mama turned a stern face to her daughters. "Close the kitchen door, girls. Now!"

Joan pushed Kiki into the kitchen, snapping the door shut behind them. "Hey!" Kiki started to protest, then changed her mind. *Maybe it can wait.* She went to the wood-burning stove, lifted one of the cast-iron lids and stoked the embers of the morning's fire. After Joan set the kettle of water on the stove's back burner, both girls tiptoed back to the door and listened.

Mrs. Moore's voice was muffled. *Darn this solid wood door.* "What are they saying?" Kiki whispered.

Joan put a finger to her lips. "Ilse said something about *Herr* General Martin ... Ooh! Mama just said the General doesn't want to be involved."

Kiki relaxed slightly. *That fraulein is no match for Mama.*

Joan evidently had the same thought. She gave Kiki a relieved smile and went across the kitchen to the sputtering teapot.

Kiki wandered to the window and looked out. The yard was covered in a blanket of new snow, smooth except for dimples the size of Roland's pawprints. *Where is that dog now?* When Roland's head popped up on the other side of the glass inches from her nose, she couldn't help squealing.

"Shh!" Joan put a warning hand on Kiki's shoulder. At the sight of Roland's tongue-hanging-out grin, Joan giggled.

"Shouldn't I go out and keep him quiet?" Kiki used her most wheedling tone.

"No, you may not." Mama stood in the kitchen doorway. "Ilse and I are going to the Officer's Club. You two, go upstairs and clean your room. I won't be long." She gave Kiki her sternest look. "Under no circumstances are you to go outside." Ilse, hovering in the shadows behind Mrs. Moore, looked unusually meek. Kiki put the image in the back of her mind for later thought.

"But, Mama, ..." Joan began.

Mrs. Moore glanced at Ilse, gave Joan a warning look and reached for her coat. Moments later the two women stepped outside, closing the door behind them.

"For crying out loud!" Joan strode into the living room, watching from the window as Mama and Ilse walked briskly down the *strausse*. "If that doesn't beat all! I don't know who's the traitor, Ilse or Mama!"

"I gave up trying to understand grown-ups a long time ago." Kiki walked to the back door. "Want to take a look in the shed?" At that moment Roland pushed in past her, paws caked with mud.

"Grab him," Joan screeched, "Mama just mopped the floor!" Kiki tackled Roland and dropped to her knees, wrestling him to a stop.

When the dog's paws--and the floor--were wiped clean, Joan sat back and glared at Kiki. "You want to go out there again? Against Mama's orders? Have you already forgotten what happened last time you did that? You got attacked, remember?"

"As if I could forget!" Kiki shifted Roland's paws off her legs and got to her feet. "Things like that don't happen to you. Me? I attract trouble even when I'm behaving." *I wish I could tell her about the ghost, but Daddy made me promise.*

It was as if Joan could read her sister's mind. She frowned. "Sometimes I wonder about you." She stood and leaned against the counter. "Mama said ...." She was interrupted by a knock at the front door. Kiki and Roland dashed from the kitchen, barking and giggling.

"Stop! It could be the attackers!" Joan sounded just like Mama. Kiki and Roland both froze.

"Joan? You in there? It's us, the Browns." Harold's face

appeared in the doorway's side window.

Joan elbowed Kiki aside. "Well, it could have been bad guys." She opened the door to Harold and Peggy. "Come on in. *Welcommen.* Our parents are out and I'm in charge."

"Did you hear about the robberies?" Harold was out of breath, as if he'd run all the way from his house. "There was a string of break-ins last night, The MPs report to our dad, so we heard about them."

"*Ach du Lieber!*" Joan looked at Kiki. "Maybe it was the same people who grabbed you."

"What're you talking about?" Harold crossed the living room and dropped onto the sofa.

"What happened, Kiki?" Peggy perched next to her brother.

Kiki blushed, muttering, "It was no big deal. Someone grabbed me when I was out in our back yard. They hit Roland, too." She put a hand on the dog's head, rubbing the spot between his ears. "Those guys were lucky he didn't see them."

Harold and Peggy looked stunned. "*Gott in Himmel!*" The German swearwords rolled easily off Peggy's tongue. "In your own yard? Are you okay?"

Harold cradled Roland's furry jaw in his hands. "You protected her? *Gutt Hund.*" Good dog.

Roland cocked his ears, then jumped on the sofa and licked the boy's cheek.

"Eeww!" Harold blushed and pushed him away.

"Down, boy!" Joan and Kiki sputtered, laughing.

"Okay, enough! You need to tell us what happened, Kiki. You look okay; ditto your dog. Give us the details." Peggy sounded more impatient than concerned.

"Okay. Sorry. There's been so much going on around here, it feels good to laugh." Kiki composed herself. "I went outside after dark. We didn't finish exploring the shed yesterday afternoon, and I'm dying to see what's under that crate." She glanced at Joan. "I took Roland. I even took a flashlight. It should have been okay. I mean, it was just the back yard."

"So, you went out. Then what?" Harold sounded like a magician trying to coax a rabbit out of a hat.

"Right when I shined the flashlight on the lock—Daddy left the key in—I heard this funny 'thump,' then someone grabbed me and pulled a stinky bag over my head." She shivered. "That's all. Can we talk about something else?"

Harold and Peggy stared at her. Harold finally whispered, "But, what happened? Tell us the rest, please."

Kiki felt Joan's hand close over hers. "Okay," she whispered. "The thump was from when they hit Roland on the head. He's okay now, thank goodness. Daddy came around the house—Mama doesn't like him smoking his cigars inside—just in time." Kiki stopped talking; the room was absolutely quiet.

"I don't think it was the guy who robbed the houses two streets over." Peggy sounded hesitant, like she was thinking as she spoke. "The MPs caught him. It was a boy, smaller than me and Henry. And he just took food."

"Hold it." Harold interrupted Peggy. "You said 'them,' Kiki. Was there more than one guy?"

"Oh. I forgot to tell you." Kiki trembled, trying to push down the residue of terror. "A *fraulein* was there, too." Her voice dropped to a whisper. "It sounded like Ilse."

"Your maid? The one we saw walking with your mom just now?" Peggy shook her head. "Did you tell your parents?"

"Yes. But she said it wasn't her."

"What'd the MPs have to say?" Harold got to his feet and began pacing like a worried adult.

"We didn't report it." Joan looked defensive. "This is an Occupied area. Daddy said the MPs don't have time to babysit Army brats." She raised an eyebrow. "My sister is always getting in trouble. We're used to it. Besides, we have other stuff to worry about." She walked to the stairs. "Any chance you could help me with my math homework, Peggy? I can't make heads or tails of those geometric equations."

Peggy and Harold exchanged glances. "I guess so. Sure." Peggy followed Joan up the stairs.

"You gonna be okay, Kiki?" Harold clasped his hands together and stared at her. "Do you think someone wanted to get in the shed?"

Kiki sighed. *Finally, someone understands.* "Yes. And, it was Ilse. I recognized her voice. There must be Nazi stuff in there. Did I tell you what we found in her room? A copy of the book Hitler wrote."

Harold looked around the quiet living room. From upstairs the sound of the girls' voices ebbed and flowed. "How about we check out the shed right now?"

Mrs. Moore's words, "Under no circumstances should you go outside," echoed in Kiki's brain. *If Mama finds out, she'll be so disappointed in me.* Kiki shook her head. *I'll hurry. We'll just be a few minutes.* She snapped her fingers to Roland. "Let's get some fresh air."

When they stepped onto the back porch, the terror resurfaced. *The bad guys are gone,* Kiki reassured herself. *It's daytime. Harold is with me.* She put a tentative hand on her friend's back and went down the steps.

CHAPTER FOURTEEN

When her fingers touched the shed door a shiver ran along Kiki's spine. She felt, again, the rough hands grabbing her. She looked blindly around, gasping for air.

"You okay, Kiki?" Harold touched her shoulder lightly. "What's up?"

"No!" came out in a squeak. Kiki dropped to her knees, grabbing Roland around the neck. The dog stopped sniffing at the shed door and stood, statue-like, while she buried her face in his fur.

"Should we go back inside? This is my fault. I should have my head examined. I forgot about what happened to you out here."

"'s okay," Kiki muttered. "I want to do this." She got to her feet. "Just stay close, okay?" She tried, unsuccessfully, to smile.

When Harold opened the shed door Roland bounded in first, whining excitedly. Kiki's flashlight lit up a triangular, cobweb-framed section of the sour-smelling outbuilding.

It's just like we left it. Kiki felt herself relax. "Look in the crate, Harold. See those hinges?"

Harold lifted the wooden lid and peered in. "You think the bottom lifts up?" He shivered and turned away. "Maybe this isn't such a good idea."

Kiki put her shoulder against the edge of the crate. It didn't budge. "Oof. This thing's heavy."

"I changed my mind. Let's not do this, at least not without your dad." Harold edged toward the outside door. "I mean, who knows what's down there? What if it's a trap?" His eyes looked huge in the flashlight's flickering gleam.

I can't believe he's chickening out. Kiki looked around the shed, spotting her father's tool box. "Maybe there's a crowbar in there." Harold didn't move. She sighed. "Who knows when Daddy will have time for this. I just want to see what's down there, okay? Don't be scared."

"*Gott in Himmel!* Harold's forehead shone with perspiration. "I'm not scared; well, maybe a little. But, dammit, Kiki it's disrespectful. You wouldn't understand: you're not Jewish."

"What do you mean, disrespectful?" Kiki snapped. "I respect people. Not everything is about people's religion."

"Here in Germany, it is." Harold rubbed his face. "Jews—people—went into hiding from the Gestapo. Someone might've died down there."

Kiki took a good look at this teen-aged boy who had befriended her. He was sweating, and his hair was standing up in clumps. *Do I tell him about the little ghost? No.* "Just a quick look. Please?"

"Rats live in cellars. You do know they carry bubonic plague?" Harold stared miserably into the darkness.

"Can't we just have a quick look-see?" Kiki tried to keep the pout out of her voice.

Harold shook his head. "I forget what a child you are. See you later." He opened the door and stepped outside.

Kiki didn't move. She heard the crunch of his sneakers on the back steps, heard the kitchen door open and close. *I'm by myself, in the shed.* She became aware of the cold, damp floor, the stale, cobwebby air and the pervasive, persistent gloom. She stood, put a hand on the doorknob. *Darn that Harold.*

She glanced at Roland. He was crouched next to the crate, sniffing along the bottom edge. "You still want a look, boy?"

Woof! Roland's black lips pulled back in a grin.

"Me, too." Kiki aimed the flashlight at the tool box. "Let's see what's in there." Minutes later she had the claw end of Daddy's hammer under the crate. **CRACK!** The board gave way. "We got it!" She fell back, smiling.

Roland, tail wagging, nosed into the opening and then backed away. A stale, putrid smell drifted out.

"Eeew! It's been closed up way too long." Kiki covered her nose with her sleeve and aimed the flashlight into the dark hole.

She saw, first, what looked like the top of a ladder, then slats down to a dirt floor. *Probably just a root cellar.* Without thinking she took a deep breath; and gagged. *Gotta hold my nose.* By moving the light back and forth she saw shelves stacked with boxes on three walls, cots on the fourth wall. When the light touched a blanket on one of the cots, something moved.

Fear swept over Kiki; she closed her eyes, becoming aware of Roland's warm, slightly rough paw on her arm. *Okay. We can do this.*

She adjusted the flashlight for a better look at the cots: One was bare canvas stretched between poles; the other was covered by a blanket. When the light touched on something round and pale at the end of the blanket, Kiki almost quit breathing. *Is that a human skull?* She flashed back to her other experience with human remains, at the abandoned house in Napa. A year before

Colonel Moore was sent to Germany, Kiki's family moved to their ranch in the Browns Valley section of Napa, California. The property had two houses, one small and run-down, one just a burned-out shell. It was in the attic of the burned-out house that Kiki found her first skeleton.

Now, half-way around the world, the terror of that experience was still fresh. Kiki went limp—the flashlight dropped into the cellar—and leaned against Roland. Her whole body trembled. *I have to get out of here.* Carefully, robotically, she pulled the crate back over the cellar opening.

Roland cocked his head, watching her. He made a small **Woof!** and padded to the outside door.

Kiki followed him, opening the door and looking all around before dashing across the yard. When they reached the kitchen door she whispered, "Good boy," feeling suddenly cold as ice.

"About time you came in. Peggy and I have to get going." Harold opened the kitchen door and stood back as Kiki and Roland stumbled in. "You look under the crate?"

Kiki stared blankly at him. Then, "You were right," burst from her. She covered her face with her hands.

"About what?" Harold's voice cracked. "The cellar? You got in there? *Gott in Himmel!*" His chair scraped across the linoleum. "Joan," he croaked. "Kiki needs you!"

Kiki looked between her fingers as Joan and Peggy hurried into the kitchen, giggling. "What's going on?" Joan saw her sister's face and stopped laughing.

This is what a cornered animal feels like. Kiki groaned. She'd gone in the shed--*verboten*--opened the cellar door without adult supervision--*verboten*--and found something awful. "I'm gonna throw up." She pushed back her chair and ran from the kitchen.

"What in the world?" Peggy glared at Harold. "Don't give me that innocent smirk, little brother. What did you do?"

"Nothing," Harold squeaked. Beads of sweat popped out on

his forehead. "I did nothing. We went outside; the dog wanted out." He ran a hand across his jaw. "I came back in. They didn't. Now she's all weird and upset."

The older girls studied him, frowning. "I know when you're lying," Peggy said. "You're not lying, but you're not telling the whole truth, either."

Harold darted a quick look at his sister. "Kiki's been through a lot, you guys. So, she was outside on her own a few minutes. So, she might've looked in the shed. So, big deal. Give her a break."

Joan groaned. "The shed? She was in there again, after what happened last night? You gotta be kidding!" She turned to Peggy. "You have no idea what it's like, being in a family with a crazy sister." Her lower lip trembled theatrically.

Peggy smirked. "Try living with this guy a few days!" She rolled her eyes at Harold.

Harold didn't return the smile. "It goes both ways. Peggy." He turned his pale, blotchy face to Joan. "I don't think she's crazy. It's not easy for any of us here. We army brats need to stick together."

Joan glanced at Harold, then looked away. "I know you're right. It's just, our family gets more than its share of trouble. And Kiki's always right in the middle."

"Speaking of families," Harold grabbed the chance to change the topic, "guess what? Our mom found out about the people who lived in our house before us. Keen, huh?"

"That's right," Peggy chimed in. "The Bad Kissengen courthouse was bombed, but someone saved the town records. The people who owned our house were musicians. They had concerts on the lawn in the summer."

Joan's face lit up. "Ask her about our house, would you? I've been wondering if it belonged to Ilse before the war--she acts like it did."

"Okay." Peggy nudged her brother. "It's time we got

going."

"*Jah, jah.*" Harold glanced at Joan. "You gonna check on the kid?"

Joan sighed. "*Jah.*" She headed for the stairs. As the Browns left Peggy called out, "Feel better, Kiki."

When Joan came into the bedroom she found Kiki sitting on the floor, staring at her fingernails.

"You okay? Harold said you went in the shed." Joan knelt next to Kiki, frowning. "What happened this time? You didn't get grabbed again, did you?"

When Kiki ignored her, Joan draped an arm around her sister's shoulder and whispered, "You're not the only one with problems. I'm worried about a ton of things."

"Huh." Kiki looked up. "Like what, your complexion? Your hair?" She pulled impatiently at her frizzy, growing-out perm. "I heard you say I'm crazy. Thanks a lot." She got to her feet and walked from the room, slamming the door behind her.

"Come downstairs, girls. We need to talk." Mama's voice was tense. "Your father's been called away on maneuvers but he'll be back in a few days."

Kiki looked over the upstairs railing at Mrs. Moore standing in the foyer, her coat, scarf and boots dusted with snow, and yelled, "Joan, Mama's back!"

In the kitchen minutes later, Mama warming her hands over the stove and the girls perched nervously at the table, Joan ventured, "Did Daddy get in trouble? Did you talk to the General about Ilse?"

Mama's shoulders stiffened. The face she turned to the girls was tear-streaked. "He's not in trouble. Maneuvers are a normal part of his work." She hesitated. "Ilse's going to another family. We're getting a *fraù* named Gisela." Her mouth formed a firm line. "From now on, you're to be on your best behavior. No tricks, no misbehaving."

Joan and Kiki nodded. "Yes, Mama."

"The new *frau* won't do overnights." Mama paused. "I know you two thought you were being loyal to me concerning Ilse, but you made things much worse." She clasped her hands together tightly. "When we were in Napa and your father was here, we were on our own. This is not so different. Here in Germany, his work leaves almost no time for us." This was a very long speech for Mama. When it ended, she turned away from the girls, her shoulders drooping.

Daddy won't be home for a few days? What about the cellar? Kiki felt tears behind her eyelids. *Mustn't cry. Gotta be strong for Mama.* She left the table and shyly wrapped her arms around her mother's waist. Joan, too, crossed the room to kiss Mama's cheek, saying, "We're sorry. We'll try to do better."

That evening, when Kiki and Joan were both in bed and Joan was asleep, Kiki lay awake worrying. *Why did Daddy have to go on maneuvers? With him away, who can I tell about what I saw in the shed?* She slipped off the bed and knelt on the cold wood floor. "Jesus," she prayed, "I said my prayers a while ago. Got another minute? People call you the 'Holy Ghost.' Do you have power over other ghosts? If you do, please tell that little boy to go to heaven where he belongs. And, while you're at it, make him leave me alone. I'm just a kid; I can't help him. Amen."

She'd been back in bed just a few minutes when, **BOOM!**

Thunder shook the house. Within seconds rain pounded on the roof.

Scratch, Scratch!

Kiki froze. From under the covers she watched, terrified, as the door creaked open. A dark form pushed into the room and hurtled onto the bed, landing at her feet. It was Roland, wild-eyed and whining.

Another **BOOM!** resounded from above the house; the frightened dog scrambled over the top of Kiki and burrowed deep beneath the bedcovers.

"Oh, my gosh! A big boy like you, afraid of a little thunder? You poor thing!" From the other side of the bed Joan mumbled, "Go to sleep."

Hours later Kiki opened her eyes and stared into Roland's ear. *Was he here all night? Oh, yeah. The thunderstorm.* She nudged the still slumbering dog. "Storm's over. Get out of our bed before Mama catches you!"

CHAPTER FIFTEEN

The kitchen's cuckoo clock made its usual grinding noise as the bird popped out, cuckooed once and popped back inside its wooden house. It was 7:30 a.m. and Kiki was still at the table, pushing powdered scrambled eggs around a white, Army-issue plate. "Do I have to eat these, Mama? I won't get hungry later, I promise."

Mama, at the stove pouring coffee from the aluminum pot, ignored her. Kiki palmed a handful of the unappetizing stuff and held it under the table. When Roland's nose, then his wet, sandpapery tongue touched her hand, she smiled. "All done. May I be excused?"

Mrs. Moore, coffee mug in hand, glanced under the table. "You gave him your breakfast? Do I have to remind you about the children starving in India?" A frown appeared on Mama's porcelain-smooth face.

"I have a tummy ache." Kiki tried to look pathetic. "Maybe I should stay home from school." When Mama didn't answer Kiki added, "Besides, Roland was SO scared in last night's storm."

Mama crossed the kitchen to put a hand under Kiki's chin, staring into her eyes. "You don't look sick." She glanced at Roland, now licking his paws. "Poor thing probably thought we were being bombed. We mustn't forget he's a war veteran." She put Kiki's plate in the sink. "Go brush your teeth. Your ride will be here any minute."

Peggy and Harold's mother had car pool duty. When their jeep stopped at the front gate, Kiki hung back as long as possible. When she climbed in she was careful not to make eye contact with anyone.

They headed down *Vierstraùsse*, Mrs. Brown glancing at them through the rearview mirror. "Where are your manners, Peggy? A friendly greeting is in order." She cut her eyes to Harold, slouched in the passenger seat. "You, too, young man. Cat got your tongue? Last I heard, the Moore girls were your friends."

Harold lifted his chin a notch. "*Guten morgen,*" he muttered.

"*Ja, guten morgen.*" Peggy sounded slightly more convincing. "We just saw each other last night, Mom. And we have a lot on our minds."

At that, Harold's head came up. He glanced at Kiki. "Right. *Ja wol.* Uh, Mom, can you find out who used to live at the Moores'? Like you did for our place?"

"That's right." Joan spoke up cheerfully. "We have to write an essay comparing Bad Kissengen with our homes in the States. It would help SO much to know something about our *Vierstraùsse house.*"

Kiki turned her head just enough for a quick glance at the others. *What are they up to? Could they possibly be trying to help me?*

Mrs. Brown's eyebrows went up. "An essay? First I've heard. Oh, what can it hurt? All right. I'll look into it." She gave Peggy, then Harold, the eagle eye in the rearview mirror. "Teenagers, I swear."

When the jeep pulled up to the school's ornate marble pillars, Kiki was first out. Calling back, "Thanks, Mrs. Brown," she took the steps two at a time and hurried inside.

Joan's, "Kiki! Wait up!" was lost in the babble of students milling around outside the school. Kiki went directly to her assigned place at the long table, got a notebook and pencil from her book bag and stared at the paper. *If anyone talks to me, I'll act like I don't hear them, like I'm studying.* She almost smiled at the thought. No one studied at this pitiful excuse for a school. She wrote,

March 10, 1947 Kiki Moore

*Now what? I wish I could write about the cellar. I can't, though. The wrong person might read it. Who would that be, the wrong person? If that body's been there a long time—and it probably has, since it's nothing but bones—*Kiki shuddered. *The wrong people would be any Germans.* She put down her pencil. *So, why'd they grab me? To keep me from going in the shed and finding the body? I don't think so. There are probably dead bodies all over Germany right now. Maybe someone wanted to hold me for ransom.*

The thought chilled her. It couldn't be true. The Moores weren't rich. She lifted her head and looked around. Students stood in small groups, talking quietly. Miss Rose, in the doorway, looked adoringly up at a handsome lieutenant.

Without warning, these mundane realities dissolved into chaos: the room's walls tilted; people screamed; booming sounds came from outside. A child's voice shrieked, *"Wo ist*

Mama?"

Kiki froze. *This can't be happening!* She closed her eyes, concentrated on breathing. Gradually the noise faded. The room stopped shaking.

"Sis? You okay?" Joan's voice, close to Kiki's ear.

Kiki felt Joan's breath next to her cheek. She opened her eyes. Just beyond Joan, Miss Rose's bright green wool jacket came into focus.

"Is your sister having a fit? No one told me she did that." Miss Rose's voice was unusually high-pitched, almost squeaky.

I've scared her. That bombing wasn't real, no one heard it —felt it—but me. Kiki ran a hand across her face and stood, pushing away from the table. "I'm okay. I just need a drink of water." She turned and ran from the room.

The broad, marble hallway in this ornate building was equipped with old-fashioned, copper and porcelain water fountains. Kiki put her face right next to the spigot and twisted the copper handle. Water, icy cold, bubbled out. It stung her eyes, her cheeks, her nose.

"Aagh!" She gasped, shaking her head. Then, using her sleeve as a towel, she wiped her face and walked out through the carved wooden entry doors into the cold morning.

She crossed the cobblestone square to a narrow, shadowed alley and leaned against a stone wall, hands jammed into her pockets. She looked across to the undamaged, solid structure she'd just left.

Did we have an earthquake? No. There's no damage, and the only person who felt it was me. Joan, Miss Rose, everyone else was fine, no problem. Maybe I'm going crazy. Either that or ....

She dropped to the ground and sat with her back against the wall.

It's like my ghost-sighting is pushing me into the past, to before the war ended. Kiki shuddered, remembering the earsplitting BOOM, the walls tipping, and .... *a child's voice. I heard a child calling for his mother. Oh, no! Was it the ghost boy from the shed? Was I experiencing what happened to him?* She wrapped her arms around her legs and rested her head on her knees. *I need Daddy. He'd understand. He'd know I'm not crazy.*

She looked across the street at the school. *I can't go back in there. They'll all laugh at me. Should I go home? No. We promised Mama we'd be extra good and here I am, a school runaway.*

The school building's ornately carved double doors opened. A man in uniform stepped out. Kiki held her breath. *Is that ... could that be ... Daddy?* The man was about the same size as Colonel Moore, the same dark hair and ruddy skin. Kiki got to her feet. As she raised her arm to wave, the weak winter sun touched bars on the man's shoulder: lieutenant's bars. *Not Daddy.* Kiki's arm dropped to her side. She shrank back into the shadows. *That's the lieutenant Miss Rose was flirting with. Is he coming after me? Will they put me in the stockade for ditching school?*

Kiki got to her feet. Staying in the shadows, she walked the length of the alley to a wide, quiet *strasse*. Looking out at the clean, sunny street, she remembered Daddy's warning: 'In Germany, you girls are not safe outside alone.' *I should go back to school.* She stepped out of the alley and onto the sidewalk, feeling visible and unprotected.

"*Guten morgen, jung fraùlein.*" An old woman, scarcely taller than Kiki and bent over with a bundle of sticks on her back, gave her a toothless, wrinkled smile.

"*Guten morgen.*" Kiki thrust a hand into her pocket and pulled out the half of a Hershey bar she'd been saving for snack time. "*Du bist* hungry?"

The watery eyes beneath the woman's black headscarf lit up. She reached out a bony, claw-like hand and snatched the candy. *"Danke Schòn."* She stuffed the candy in her pocket and hurried away.

Kiki walked on, feeling marginally better. *That was a nice thing to do. Maybe that old lady won't hate Americans so much, now.* A few yards farther along she saw the fir trees, rose bushes and benches that marked the village square. *There's the statue Daddy jokes about--the one of the little naked boy peeing. Maybe I'll sit on that bench for a minute.*

As she stepped off the curb to cross the street a jeep rounded the corner. She jumped back into the shadows and watched it roar past. It was an MP jeep.

Are they looking for me? A voice in Kiki's head—Joan's voice—said, "No. You're not that important. It's not like ditching school is against the law." Kiki sighed. *I should go back. It's no fun feeling like a criminal. Bui how can I be sure that nightmare won't happen again? Is there something strange about that building, or maybe that room? That's never happened before. What's changed?*

She turned and walked aimlessly back along the street. At the alley's arched entrance, she turned for a final look toward the park. *Mama says someone should put pants on that boy.* She smiled. Glancing toward a *roasthaus* next to the park, Kiki saw a blonde woman in a bright red head scarf chatting with an American officer. *Who is that?* The woman's coat—red wool— looked familiar. *That's Mama's coat, the one she lost last week!* The woman looked familiar, too. Her posture, her height—it was Ilse.

Kiki ducked into the alley and stood there a minute, trying to make sense of what she'd seen. *Maybe it's not Mama's coat. Yes, it is. I recognize the fur collar and cuffs. Who is that man? Not Daddy. He's way taller than Daddy. Did Ilse steal Mama's coat? Has she seen me?* She thought of the attack outside the shed two nights earlier, suddenly terrified. *The voice I heard was Ilse's. I have to get away from here.* She ran back down the alley, tripping, stumbling, running on. Finally, out of breath and with a stitch in her side, she dropped to the ground.

"Sorry I ditched you yesterday."

Kiki lifted her head, not sure someone had really spoken. Harold leaned in a doorway a few feet from her. He wasn't smiling—he looked worried.

Kiki blinked, took a second look. "Is school out already?"

"No, Nitwit." Harold's long legs crossed the alley in two steps. "When Joan couldn't find you in the building, I asked Miss Rose to let me look outside. "You okay?"

Relief overwhelmed Kiki. She began to cry, then swiped angrily at the tears. "No, I'm not okay!" burst from her involuntarily. "Sorry, Harold. It's not your fault. Will I be expelled?"

"For what, being quiet? For getting lost on your way to the water fountain?" Harold eased down onto the step next to Kiki. "Is this about what you saw in the shed? I'm still waiting to hear about that."

"Yeah, kind of." Kiki couldn't bring herself to look at this nice American who happened to be a boy. She put a hand over her mouth and muttered, "I can't go back in there. I need my dad."

"Huh?" Harold leaned in a little. "Your dad? How come?" He made a steeple of his fingers. "Maybe if you started at the beginning, I'd get it." He raised his eyebrows and gave Kiki a crooked grin.

"Daddy's the only one who understands." *Oh, no, have I said too much? Will the army find out about what Daddy calls our sixth sense? He told me never to tell anyone.* She got to her feet. "I'm okay now. Let's go back." She forced herself to walk out of the alley and across the street.

"Hold up! At least tell me about the shed before we go back to class." Harold caught up with Kiki and put a restraining hand on her arm.

Darn him, anyway! "All right, but cross your heart and hope to die you won't tell anyone." Kiki glared up at Harold. "There's a room under the shed. And a dead body, a small one that's been there a long time."

CHAPTER SIXTEEN

Harold must have been holding his breath, because he let it out with a whoosh. "Holy cow!" He stared at Kiki. "Did your dad report it? Is that why you spaced out in class? Why you took off? You look awful. Maybe you should have stayed home today."

"He didn't report it. He's away on maneuvers. I haven't told anyone." Kiki looked at Harold. *He can't help me. I'm scaring him.* "Listen: Thanks for coming out to look for me. I'm okay now. Keep what I told you a secret, okay? Just 'til my dad gets back." She twisted her face into what she hoped was a reassuring smile and gripped the school's door handle.

"Hold on! You sure you want to go back in there? You might have another fit."

He's right, but what choice do I have? Kiki stepped back. Keeping her voice low, she said, "No, Harold; I'm not sure. You got any other ideas?"

"Well, yeah. As a matter of fact, I do. But first, tell me what happened in there."

Kiki frowned. "I don't know, okay? That's the problem. It's grown-up stuff, and I'm not grown up. You aren't, either, and you're a boy, besides."

Harold's face reddened. Kiki looked away, embarrassed. *Why did I say that?*

The door opened again. Joan leaned out, hissing, "There you are! Get in here. Miss Rose finally noticed you're gone, and she's in a tizzy!"

"Big stupid deal," Harold muttered. Without looking at either of them, he pushed past Joan and went inside.

"What's going on?" Joan watched Harold leave. "You made him mad? Are you totally nuts? He's your only friend. Why'd you ditch class? Mama and Daddy will kill you. If, that is, there's anything left when Miss Rose gets through!" She snapped her mouth shut, then leaned forward, nose-to-nose with Kiki. "What in H-E-double toothpicks is wrong with you?"

Kiki had no easy answer. She felt like she was two years old. She couldn't look at Joan. "It's like in Napa," she whispered. "In the attic of the old house." *Do I have to spell it out for her?* "Could you ask Miss Rose to go easy on me?"

Joan shook her head. "Napa? I didn't understand you then, and I still don't. She stepped back into the hallway. "C'mon. Let's get this over with."

Kiki looked through the half-open door, seeing the polished wood floors and the high-ceilinged, dimly lit hall with its shadowy corners. She gulped. *I can't do it.* She turned and ran, taking the steps two at a time.

"Come back here!" Joan screamed..

Running partly to escape the school building, partly to get away from Joan, Kiki was around the corner and on an unfamiliar street when she felt a stitch in her side. *I need to stop and catch my breath.*

As she slowed to a walk she became aware of her surroundings: snow-covered yards behind rusty iron fences; bare-branched, skeletal trees; abandoned-looking houses with shuttered, blind windows. Farther along the street, a broken lamp post leaned at a crazy angle.

She looked back, surprised at how far she'd run. She shivered, remembering the coat, scarf and mittens still hanging on their hook in the classroom. *Where am I, anyway? I've never been to this part of town.*

The boarded-over storefronts, barred doors and crookedly hanging signs spoke a clear message: 'We're dead and you will be, too, if you stick around. Go away.' Kiki walked faster. *Where am I going? Which way is home?*

At the next corner she noticed a wayside shrine, a small, open-fronted altar built into someone's stone fence. These miniature chapels fascinated Kiki. Back home she'd never seen one; here, in Germany, they seemed to be everywhere. *Mama says they're for travelers, a place to say your prayers when you're on the road. I wonder why the Nazis didn't get rid of them? Maybe they thought they were too small to bother with.* She walked up to the shrine, looking in at an undamaged statue of Jesus's mother, arms outspread and smiling. Kiki felt the welcome in that gesture, the soothing in the Virgin Mary's gentle smile. She smiled back.

As she stared, eyes unfocused, something moved in the branches of a tree behind the shrine. *What?*

A tiny brown bird poked its beak out of a knot hole, then hopped along the branch on spindly yellow legs. Turning its head from side to side, it preened its feathers and cocked a beady, black-eyed gaze at Kiki.

She didn't move; she hardly breathed. The bird blinked, then opened its shimmering, green-tinted wings and flew straight to the top of the tree. It paused there, gave a **Chirp,** and disappeared into the pale gray sky.

She watched it go, thinking, *Maybe German birds don't hate us.* She stepped off the curb and hurried along the cobblestone path.

Across the street and around the far corner, almost out of sight, a spot of bright color caught Kiki's eye. Standing out as it did from the area's lifeless greys and browns, it welcomed her. She stepped around potholes and dirty snow and hurried toward it.

Gradually her pace slowed. The color, now visible as orangish-red, came from a sign painted on the wall of a building. *It's a store.* She remembered Daddy's warning: *Stay away from Germans.*

Viewed from the street, the store's interior was dark. When Kiki reached the glass-paned door, though, she saw a dimly-lit bulb hanging over the counter. The sign behind the door's glass said *OFFEN*, printed in big, swirly letters. *That means open.*

As Kiki turned the worn brass knob and stepped in, a bell tinkled. The thin, stooped old man behind the counter raised his head and stared at her. *"Guten tag. Kinder. Du bist ein American?"*

"Ja, Ja," Kiki's eyes widened. The man's narrow black mustache was an odd contrast to the steely gray hair draped across his forehead. She was reminded of pictures of Hitler. *It can't be him. Hitler's not old. And Daddy says he's dead.* She looked at the floor, stammering, *"Wie komme ich nach Vierstrausse?* How do I get to Vier Street?"

The man's eyes, yellow and watery behind coke-bottle thick glasses, blinked. He shook his head.

He doesn't understand me. Maybe I didn't say it right. *"Vierstrausse. Meine haus?"* Kiki shivered as the store's heat—marginal though it was—flowed over her.

The man nodded, but returned to his reading. Kiki stood still, fighting an urge to run back outside. With an odd, sighing sound, the man looked up. *"Telefon?"* He pointed to the wooden box on the wall. *"Ein* dollar American."

Kiki's *"Ja!* Telephone!" trailed off when she pulled nothing but a few German coins out of her pocket. She held the brass and copper coins in her hand, palm up.

"Nein." The man shook his head and went back to his reading.

"Sir, *Herr* Storekeeper, ..." Kiki looked around desperately. A large map of Bad Kissengen hung on the wall behind the counter.

"Could you show me how to get to *Vierstrausse? Wo bist Vierstrausse?"* She dug in her pocket, pulling out the other half of her Hershey bar.

The man eyed the candy, mustache twitching. *"Ja, ja. Vierstrausse."* He picked up a pointer and indicated a spot on the wall map. *"Vierstrausse."* He opened his mouth in a toothless grin. "Now, *chocalata?"*

Kiki leaned over the counter, squinting at the map's tiny words. "Where are we?" She put the candy back in her pocket.

"Ja, vol! Yes!" The pointer zig-zagged from the *Vierstrausse* dot to another, larger one labeled, *'geschafte,'* store. The man wiggled his mustache in a gap-toothed, sour-breath grin. "Chocalata, Ja?"

Kiki studied the map. *"Munichstrausse* to *Rosenstrausse* to *Liebstrausse* to *Vierstrausse. Ja vol."* She sighed—breakfast was a distant memory—and put the candy in his outstretched hand. *"Danke."* She turned and ran outside.

Munichstrausse, seen from the front of the store, didn't look much like the line on the map. Muddy, deeply rutted, and strewn with upended cobblestones, tanks and other heavy war machinery had reduced it to a ragged path.

Kiki looked along the street to the corner. *That's Rosenstrausse down there.* She glanced back through the store's glass door, saw the storekeeper leering at her. She ran like a scared rabbit, not stopping until she reached the *Rosenstrausse* street sign.

Wrapping her fingers around the sign as if it was home base, she stopped for breath and looked around. No one had followed her. *No need to be afraid. Besides, didn't someone tell me predators can smell fear?* She thought of Roland. *He was so scared last night. Could I smell his fear? No, but then, I'm not a predator.* The thought sent an additional chill along her spine.

Kiki started walking slowly along *Rosenstrausse*, a fairly busy street fronted by houses and stores. She picked her way between rocks, puddles and snowdrifts, avoiding eye contact when two old women stopped and stared at her. *Should I turn around and go back to school?*

The thought of the school, walls tilting with the noise of bombing, made her colder than she was already. *I can't go back there. I have to go home.*

Trudging along, still cold and increasingly tired, Kiki thought grimly about the distances on a map compared to real streets. *I guess an inch on a map is the same as a mile.*

Gradually the cold, her tired legs, and hunger gave way to a pressing need to pee. She glanced across the street and saw a man standing with his back to the road, peeing. She groaned. *I can't do that. Absolutely not.* She picked up her pace, trotting now and trying to think about anything but the need to pee.

Munich, Rosen, Lieb, Vier. Munich, Rosen, Lieb, Vier." As she marched to the words, the tension in her shoulders lessened. She made up a sort of hop, step, double-step dance, thinking about Daddy and how he loved music and dancing. *I do, too. Maybe I'll be a dancer when I grow up.*

Munichstrausse had been almost devoid of traffic, with only the occasional American jeep and one small boy pushing a wheelbarrow. *Rosenstrausse,* the street with the cemetery, was busier. Kiki watched as two women went through the graveyard's wrought-iron gates. They were dressed in black from head to toe. One of the women carried a holly bouquet. *Are they going to a funeral? Who's left to die?* Kiki pushed away the unkind thought.

"*Achtung, jung* American *fraulien!* Whatcha doin'? Got *zigaretten?*" This rude call came from farther along the street, at the next corner. Three German boys around Harold's age grinned and waved. *Are they calling me?* Kiki looked back, saw no one. *Yes. I'll ignore them, but is it safe to go by?* The experience of being held by rough hands, face jammed into a smelly cloth bag, flashed through her mind. She stepped off the curb and crossed the street, standing as tall as possible and forcing herself not to run.

"Where you ..." The rude voice began, then stopped. A Jeep carrying two MPs came cruising up the street. Kiki ducked behind a fence, watching as the Jeep pulled to the curb and the boys drifted away.

Her sigh of relief was followed quickly by the thought, '*Is it against the law to ditch school?*' She stood very still, praying for invisibility.

The MPs sat in the Jeep, looking around and talking. One of them pointed toward the retreating boys. After a few minutes the vehicle made a U-turn and drove away.

With no menacing boys and no MPs to worry about, Kiki walked along, letting her thoughts drift to the memory of Ilse wearing Mama's coat. *Mama only has two coats. She wouldn't give one away. Did Daddy give it to Ilse? Absolutely not; he knows Mama needs it. Ilse stole it.*

The realization stopped Kiki. She looked around, not actually seeing the houses, snow-covered gardens, low stone fences. *It was Ilse who stood by when someone tried to hurt me, made trouble for Daddy, took Mama's coat. Is Mama safe from her now, with Daddy away?* She started walking again, faster, her thoughts on months ago in Napa. *No one believed me about the danger to Mama then, either.* A sharp pain in her stomach got her attention. *I really need to pee.*

Liebstrausse, a residential street, was shorter and narrower than *Rosenstrausse.* On this street the houses looked closed-up but not abandoned. Sidewalks were cleared of snow; doors and windows were shuttered but not barred.

Kiki looked back, ahead, left and right; saw no one. *Here goes nothing.* She stepped behind a tall, wide-branched cedar bush, squatted, pulled down her britches and peed. *AAAh!* The relief was instant. Breaking off a handful of spiky, soft cedar fronds she wiped herself, pulled up her britches and stepped out onto the path.

Walking along with the confidence of someone who can take care of herself, Kiki looked carefully around. *I remember that house. Mama calls that funny roof 'thatched,' says mice live in thatched roofs.* She smiled, partly at the idea of mice making a home in someone's roof, partly from the relief of not needing to pee, but mostly because she was now in familiar territory. The thatched roof, that odd little church with the bar across its' faded double doors—she'd passed them many times on the way to school.

She started skipping, humming *'Ach du Lieber Augustine'* as she went. This catchy German drinking song, one of Daddy's favorites, was especially good for skipping. She did a little twirl, rebalanced, and looked farther down the street as a low brown-and-black shape came around the corner, nose down and sniffing. Kiki stood still. *Is that Roland? Can't be. He's not allowed out.*

Just in case it was Roland, she put her hands on either side of her mouth and called, "Roland, *Herkommen!* Come here!"

The animal lifted his head, gave a joyful bark and ran full speed toward her.

Oh, my gosh! Kiki hurried forward, then stopped. A stooped over, old woman dressed from head to toe in black stood in Roland's path, looking terrified. *He's trained to attack civilians.*

"Roland! Halt!" she yelled. *"Guten Tag, Grofsmutter. Ist meine hund."*

Roland skidded to a stop and stood still, ears forward and growling. Kiki ran past the woman and stopped in front of the him, one hand outstretched.

"It's okay, boy. I'm here. Sit!" She made the command as stern as possible. Roland's rear dropped to the ground, but the growling continued.

"Good. Now, stay."

Roland's ears relaxed. The growling stopped. Kiki slowly approached and put her arms around his furry shoulders. "Good boy," she whispered.

When she looked around, the woman was gone. "Guess she went back in her house," Kiki whispered. "Let's go home, boy."

As they turned the corner onto *Vierstrausse* Kiki said, "How did you get out, boy?" Roland, trotting alongside, flicked his ears but didn't look back.

Mama wouldn't let him out. Daddy gave strict orders about that. Ilse's stern face came into Kiki's thoughts. *Maybe Mama's not okay. Maybe Ilse came back.* Kiki looked around, trying not to panic.

The Moores' house was half a block away. In the weak rays of early afternoon sun its recently washed windows sparkled. A plume of smoke drifted up from the chimney. Kiki heard the faint, lilting notes of an accordion from the back of the house. *Is that a polka? Why is Mama listening to that? She doesn't even like polka music.*

It felt good, being so close to home. Kiki felt her shoulders relax. *It's dumb of me to worry about Mama. She probably doesn't even know Roland got out.*

"Uh, Roland? Let's go in through the back. That way maybe I can sneak upstairs without Mama knowing."

Roland turned his head, gave her a, "Are you crazy?" yawn, and stepped off the path onto the Moores' property.

Kiki came around the back corner of the house, saw the shed, and froze: the horror of being attacked caught up with her. She dropped to her knees, moaning.

Eeeii! Eeeii! Roland's anxious whimper and damp, scratchy tongue on her cheek revived her.

"Okay, boy. Okay." She pushed him away and got to her feet, careful not to look at the shed. *If I pretend it's not there, I can get in the house.* She hurried up the back steps and flung herself into the kitchen.

CHAPTER SEVENTEEN

"Du bist ein kinder? Frau Moore's kinder?"

A woman Kiki had never seen before, a German woman, stood in the doorway between the kitchen and the living room. She was tall, much taller than Daddy or Mama, and her blondish-grey hair was pulled back so tightly her eyes looked slanted. The strings of one of Mama's aprons—it was way too small on this woman—dangled loosely. The face she turned to Kiki was menacing.

"Ja. Ich bin Kiki Moore. *Was ist* your name, *fraulien? Wo ist* Mama?" Kiki knew it was rude, talking like that to an adult, but she didn't care. This woman, this stranger, was in Mama's kitchen looking right at home.

"Frau Moore *ist* out." The woman snapped. *"Zur Schule gehen. jetzt."* Go back to school, now."

Roland had lowered his hindquarters so he was sitting at Kiki's feet. When the woman spoke he stood, a low, rumbling growl coming up from his throat.

"No. I'm sick. Er, *krank.*" *I hope that's the right word.* Kiki put a calming hand on Roland's head. "Who let him out? Daddy doesn't allow that."

The woman stepped behind the table. "*Die hund flucht.* Ran away. Tie him up and return to school, *bitte.*"

"No." Kiki was tired, hungry and cold. "I will not. Where is my mother? *Wo ist mutter?*" Kiki stood tall and pushed out her flat, skinny chest in what she hoped was a warrior's pose.

The woman's face reddened. Her mouth became a thin line; her hands became fists. The words she spat out appeared to escape involuntarily. "You will not speak so to me. I am Gisela Reising, *die wirtschafterin*--the housekeeper. *Herr* colonel will be ..." she paused in search of English words, "informed of your behavior."

This startled Kiki. *She's our new maid? Oh, boy. I'm in trouble now. Where's Mama? Why did she leave a stranger in charge?* She said, speaking slowly and with as much authority as she could manage, "*Ja vol.* I'll tell him you let Roland run away."

The woman's mouth closed in that tight, thin line.

Now what? Did she even understand me? "When Mama--*die mutter*--comes back, tell her I'm upstairs." With eyes on the woman Kiki moved woodenly across the kitchen to the ice box, took out the milk bottle and, hands shaking, poured a glass of milk. She emptied the glass in one gulp, grabbed an oatmeal cookie from the jar and headed for the stairs. Roland, still keeping himself between Kiki and the maid, managed to push his nose into the hand holding the cookie.

At the top of the stairs Kiki turned, looking down into the kitchen. Gisela stood watching, grim-faced. Kiki hurried into the bedroom and slammed the door.

"I really did it this time." She sat on the floor next to Roland, nibbling on the cookie. "What do you think, boy? Was that Gisela woman telling the truth? Would Mama leave with a new maid in the house?" She put a piece of cookie in the palm of her hand for Roland.

It doesn't add up. Roland wouldn't run away. He's trained to protect Mama and the house.

Kiki stood and began pacing the room, following the triangular pattern on the rug. *Maybe I'm worrying over nothing: Maybe Mama showed Gisela the house, then went to a bridge game. Maybe Roland just got out.*

Soothed by these thoughts, Kiki flopped down on the bed and closed her eyes. The horror of bombs hitting the school building immediately washed over her. She sat up, trembling. *That wasn't real, but it sure felt real. What brought it on? Am I going crazy? Daddy talks about soldiers being shell-shocked, reliving war experiences as if they're still happening. Did I relive someone else's experience?* The thought chilled her. For the umpteenth time she wished her father was here. He would have an answer. He understood.

"I'm on my own until Daddy gets back." She spoke into the silent room. At the sound of her voice Roland lifted his head and thumped his tail on the floor.

Things are getting worse---much worse. First the little ghost, then ghost energy, now a ghostly bombing! How can I make this stop? She left the bed and went to the window, leaning on the wooden sill and gazing vacantly down into the yard. *Back home in Napa, the ghost disappeared when the murder was solved. Could that work here? If I find out how the little boy died, will his ghost go away?*

In the yard below, movement on the far side of the shed caught Kiki's attention. That part of the back yard was dense with the tangled, bare limbs of bushes and trees, but from behind a pile of slushy snow Kiki could see the yellow, black, and red-patterned cloth of a coat sleeve. *Someone's back there.*

She stepped behind the curtain and watched as a man moved from within the foliage to the side of the shed. *Oh, no!* Kiki's first impulse was to duck out of sight and hide. She fought that and watched the muscular, dark-haired man walk quickly to the back porch and call, "*Guten tag*, Gisela!"

He's the one who attacked me! He's going inside! Kiki struggled for control as every nerve in her body screamed, **Run! Run!**

"Roland," she whispered. "Psst!" The dog lifted his head again and gave her a sleepy look. "We have to get out of here."

She thought of her parents' bedroom, with its windows overlooking the trees on that side of the house. "Can you climb down a tree?"

The dog cocked his head and yawned, showing sharp white teeth and a pink tongue.

"Let's go, boy." Kiki pulled on a wooly, hooded sweater— *I've been cold enough today*—slipped into her boots and tiptoed from the room, Roland trotting silently at her side.

As they crossed the hall, the sound of voices floated up from the kitchen. *Gisela's talking to that man. She knows him.*

Kiki put a finger to her lips—Roland had begun quietly whining—and opened her parents' bedroom door. Carefully, quietly, she and Roland stepped inside.

This room was large, twice the size of the one Joan and Kiki shared. It was dominated by a tall, dark-wood wardrobe standing next to the four-poster bed. Mama's red, white and blue flag-patterned patchwork quilt provided the only bit of color. Kiki glanced around nervously. *I shouldn't be in here. This is off limits for Joan and me.*

"C'mon, Roland." The dog, sniffing the wardrobe's bulbous wooden feet, looked up at her. "Do you smell Daddy?"

As she tiptoed to the window Kiki noticed Mama's half-open pocketbook on the floor by the bed. *That's odd. Why didn't she take it with her?* As she bent down to pick up the small leather purse, she glanced under the bed. *No dust balls. And nothing else.*

Roland pushed in next to Kiki, growling low in his throat. Without warning he wrapped his jaws around her coat sleeve and pulled her out from under the bed.

"What …?" Kiki became aware of silence from the kitchen below. Then, *"Ja vol, liebschen,"* came clearly from the stairway. The man was coming upstairs.

We have to get out. Now. Kiki tip-toed to the window, praying it would open. She pushed against it, hard. It slid up with a groan.

Roland stood next to her, his front paws on the sill. "Ready, boy?" She pointed to the tree outside the window. "Jump!" He sprang through the open window, teetered for a second on a big branch, and dropped to the ground.

The bedroom doorknob rattled. Kiki climbed onto the window ledge, pushed off and flung herself at the tree. She grabbed a branch, swung to a lower one and dropped down onto a patch of snow. With a glance at her scratched palms, she held up her fingers in a 'V' for Victory. "C'mon, boy. Run like H-E-double toothpicks!"

Luckily, the fence surrounding the Moore's yard was old and rotting. Kiki pulled apart two boards hanging by rusty nails and they scrambled through. Then, using shrubs next to the house for cover, she crept around to the front yard. At the porch, she looked back. *Where's Roland?*

The front door opened. Gisela looked out. *"Was ist los?"* What is wrong? She sounded angry.

Kiki held her breath. *Don't show yourself now, Roland!*

After an agonizingly long minute the door snapped shut. *Did she go back inside?* Kiki didn't dare look. She heard no footsteps on the porch, nothing to indicate a person standing there. Then with a flash of fur Roland was next to her, wiggling happily. Kiki gave him a quick hug and ran, crouching, across the snowy grass and out to the street.

At the corner she stopped. Roland, ahead of her, turned and came back. "We have to decide where we're going. I'm done with aimless wandering." She looked back up Vierstrausse to her family's house sitting benignly behind the snow-capped hedge. *Home's not safe anymore. Neither is school. And where is Mama?*

Kiki felt like crying. She looked down at Roland. *There has to be somewhere safe for us. There just has to be.*

A Jeep passed by, headed into town. Kiki ducked behind a telephone pole. The driver, an officer around Daddy's age, didn't look her way. *No need to worry. He wasn't looking for us.*

Harold's face, its crooked smile and freckles, popped into her thoughts. *I shouldn't have yelled at him.. It's not his fault he doesn't understand what's going on. Wait a minute: maybe we could go to the Browns.' I know the way, and Mrs. Brown likes us.*

She walked around the corner, then stopped. *What if she tells me I have to go back to school?*

Roland looked up at her. "We'll just have to convince her, won't we, boy? She probably knows where Mama is. Those officers' wives stick together." She shook the leash. "Let's go."

When they reached the street where Harold and Peggy lived, Kiki saw exhaust fumes coming from the driveway. *Mrs. Brown is leaving!*

"Mrs. Brown!" Kiki yelled, waving her arms frantically.

The Jeep backed out of the driveway and stopped. The driver turned and stared at Kiki.

Kiki slowed to a walk, suddenly self-conscious.

"Kiki Moore? What are you doing here? Didn't you go to school today?" It was Mrs. Brown, and she sounded irritated.

"I got sick," Kiki croaked. "I had to leave early. I went home, but Mama's not there." She gulped. "Our new maid wouldn't let me stay home. Can I stay with you 'til my mother gets back?"

"You're sick?" Mrs. Brown shut off the ignition and climbed out of the Jeep. "Let's have a look at you." She put a hand on Kiki's forehead. "You don't have a fever. How's your tummy?"

"Okay. I mean, it doesn't hurt. I'm not that kind of sick." Kiki looked sideways at Mrs. Brown. *Here goes nothing.*

Mrs. Brown took a step back, looking puzzled. "Uh, huh. A different kind of sick. The kids mentioned you get upset easily. Something happen at school?"

Kiki nodded, felt herself relaxing, then caught herself. *Be careful. If you tell her the truth, she'll think you're crazy.*

"Yes. I started getting scary memories and had to leave."

"Were you excused by the teacher?"

There it was, the big question. Did Kiki have permission to be here, in Mrs. Brown's driveway? If Mrs. Brown helped her, would it be aiding and abetting a criminal? Kiki sighed. "No," she whispered. "Miss Rose wouldn't understand. No one understands."

Mrs. Brown leaned against the Jeep. "How did you get home?"

"Walked. I got lost and had to look on the map in a store." Kiki turned away. *She's not going to help me.* "C'mon, Roland." She shook the dog's leash.

"Wait up, Kiki." Mrs. Brown's tone was brusque. "Get in the Jeep. Put your dog in the back. I'm on my way to school anyway, to pick up the kids."

The impulse to wrap her arms around Mrs. Brown and hold

on for dear life was almost overwhelming. Kiki grinned, her first genuine grin in this very long day. She and Roland climbed in, Roland first so he could squeeze in the back. Mrs. Brown put the Jeep in gear and they drove down the street.

Kiki settled against the seat, glad for Roland's warm breath on her ear. *Should I make conversation?* Colonel Moore didn't like children bothering him while he was behind the wheel; Kiki decided it was okay to just sit quietly. She wasn't good at conversation, anyway. That was Joan's thing.

Half-way to school, Kiki felt Mrs. Brown's eyes on her in the rearview mirror. "Do my kids and your sister know why you left school?" Mrs. Brown's tone was gentle.

Kiki nodded and whispered, "Yes. Harold got permission to come outside and bring me back in."

The rearview mirror showed Mrs. Brown's raised eyebrows. "Really? My Harold? Wonders never cease! He usually doesn't know other people exist." She chuckled.

"I didn't go back, though. And now he's mad at me."

This last part got a shake of the head from Mrs. Brown. "So, your house has a new maid? When did that happen? Last I heard, the other one wasn't working out."

"Today was her first day." Kiki hoped Mrs. Brown would quit asking things. How could she tell anyone Mama had gone somewhere and left the house in the hands of bad people?

"The new maid was there and your mother wasn't? That's odd. We're supposed to give them instructions on running the household." Mrs. Brown glanced at Kiki as she maneuvered the Jeep into a parking spot. "We're not early, but we're not late, either." She smiled into the rearview mirror.

CHAPTER EIGHTEEN

"I hope Harold thanked you for giving me this charm." Mrs. Brown held up her hand and shook her wrist. The Menorah twinkled brightly among the other charms on her bracelet.

"He did, but he didn't need to. It belongs with you." Kiki blushed. *Was it okay to say that?* Lowering her voice to a whisper, she said, "Do you think its owner used to live at our house?"

"Definitely. Before the war, that place belonged to a Jewish family." Mrs. Brown glanced at Kiki. "Harold said you wanted me to check the town records."

Kiki straightened, forgetting she was in trouble. "I wonder how the charm got in our shed?" Then, answering her own question, "Maybe they hid in the bomb shelter. The family, I mean."

Mrs. Brown's smile disappeared. When she spoke, it was in a whisper. "They might have hidden from the Nazis down there.

I hope not; that's the first place Stormtroopers would look."

Kiki shivered. *Should I tell her about the ghost? Or the skeleton? No. I have to tell Daddy before anyone else..*

Just then the school door opened and students pushed out onto the broad steps. Joan emerged, carrying Kiki's backpack. She looked around, frowning into the afternoon's weak sunlight.

She looks worried. I'm in for it. Kiki called, "Joan! Over here!"

Joan's head swiveled around. Kiki saw amazement, then anger on her sister's face before another student, a gangly boy in a furry Russian *Ushanka* cap, blocked her view.

"Get out and go over to her," Mrs. Brown said quietly. It sounded like an order. Kiki climbed out, obeying automatically. As she approached the school grounds someone grabbed her arm.

"Kiki? What the hell?" It was Harold, looking sweaty and irritated.

Peggy stepped up behind him, clamping a hand on his shoulder "Cool it, little brother." She smiled at Kiki. "Glad you're okay. We were worried."

Before Kiki could answer, Joan pushed in next to Peggy. "Good grief, Kiki! Have you totally lost your mind?"

BEEP! BEEP!

Saved by the horn. Peggy and Harold both waved to their mother. With a theatrical shrug Harold turned and loped toward the Jeep. Peggy steered Joan and Kiki to the curb.

"Do I need to let Miss Rose know I'm okay?" Kiki looked back at the school.

"Just wave. See her there?" Peggy thrust her chin toward the tall leaded windows facing the street.

"Oh. Yeah." Kiki saw the dark-haired, pretty brunette looking somberly out at the mass of students. When she waved, Miss Rose nodded and turned away.

As soon as the Browns' Jeep was loaded—Harold in front, the girls in the middle and Roland standing in the back—Mrs. Brown announced, "Joan and Kiki, you're coming home with us until I can reach your mother." At her son's surly frown she added, "The Browns treat guests graciously, Harold."

"We're not going home?" Joan sounded puzzled.

I'm the reason. This is my fault. Kiki tried not to groan.

"There's been some kind of mix-up with the maid." Mrs. Brown's tone indicated no more discussion.

Joan reached back to pat Roland, whispering, "What's he doing here, Kiki? Did you go home?"

"We'll discuss it later, Joan." Mrs. Brown glanced at Harold. "I'll be especially interested in what you have to say, son."

Harold straightened, glared at Kiki, and looked out the window.

"Can I tell you I got an A on my German test, Mom?" Peggy smiled at her mother.

"Ja wohl," Mrs. Brown's eyes returned her daughter's smile.

She's mad at Harold, but not at Peggy. Just like in our house: Joan never does anything wrong and I never do anything right. Kiki studied Harold's profile as he stared out the side window. *He's actually a good friend. Even if he is a boy.*

In the Jeep, silence reigned for the remainder of the ten-minute drive. Kiki closed her eyes, trying to relax. She focused on reassuring sounds—Roland's panting, the slap-slap of the Jeep's tires on the cobblestones—but anxiety resurfaced like an ugly bubble. Her stomach churned; her forehead throbbed. She leaned forward, elbows on knees. *I have to relax; I can't lose it again. I have to hold on.*

The awful, pressured feeling in Kiki's solar plexus slowly subsided. She became aware of Joan's hand lightly covering her own, Joan's wool coat sleeve against her wrist. Kiki took a breath, letting it out as tears trickled down her cheeks.

"It's okay, honey. You're safe." Joan's breath was warm in Kiki's ear. The air in the Jeep, ominous moments ago, now sparkled with electric warmth.

Harold glanced back at Kiki and quickly looked away. "We're all on your side," He muttered. "Even dumb old me."

The Jeep made a sharp turn, swinging its passengers to the right. Roland responded with a soft yelp.

"Sorry, everyone. I almost drove past our turn." Mrs. Brown sounded embarrassed.

Minutes later, climbing from the Jeep, Joan put an arm around Kiki and half-carried her across the snow-speckled lawn.

"Can the *hund* come in, Mom?" Harold opened the front door. Before Mrs. Brown could respond, Roland bounded inside.

To Kiki, the Browns' house seemed like a palace with its broad two-story front, wrought-iron barred windows and life-sized lion statues at the front door. *This is where they live? Their dad must be really important.*

Stepping into the foyer, Kiki's first impression was of light and space. That was followed by twittering sounds and a slightly closed-up smell.

"Oh, my gosh! How adorable!" Joan handed Roland's leash to Kiki—the dog had become stiffly alert—and crossed the flagstone to an aviary filled with small, sharp-eyed blue and yellow birds.

"You wouldn't say that if you had to clean the cage." Harold grinned. "They were here when we moved in. This way to the living room." He walked away down a long, dark-paneled hall.

Joan and Kiki hurried after him, hardly noticing as Peggy

disappeared up a curved staircase. When they passed a large room that was empty except for an ebony-black grand piano Joan mumbled, "I didn't know they were musicians."

"Me, neither." *Birds? A grand piano? Who are these people? I wish they were my family.* Kiki looked wistfully around.

"Let's sit in the kitchen." Mrs. Brown opened a door at the end of the hall.

The Browns' kitchen was surprisingly small. Except for the over-large wood-burning stove and the table's red-and-white checkered cloth, it reminded Kiki of home. There was, however, one important difference: A grey-haired, rosy-cheeked woman stood at the counter lustily singing, *"O, Tannenbaum, O Tannenbaum wie true sind deine blatter,"* and stirring something in a big crockery bowl.

"Ach, Frau Brown! You have *der gesellschaft.* Er, company. I go away?" The woman smiled broadly at Kiki and Joan.

"Ja, Kristina." Mrs. Brown grinned. "First, though, let's find a snack for the *kinder."*

So, this is their maid. She looks a lot nicer than Gisela. Kiki found herself smiling at the cheerful *frau.*

Following Harold's lead—he dropped into a chair—Joan and Kiki slid self-consciously onto one of the table's built-in benches.

"Harold," Mrs. Brown opened the ice box, "get a plate for cheese and crackers. Girls, do you like Ovaltine? Harold and Peggy won't drink powdered milk any other way."

When snacks and drinks were on the table—Joan and Kiki watched as Mrs. Brown, Harold and the maid worked comfortably together—Mrs. Brown called,. "Peggy? Downstairs, on the double."

"Ich bin folding sheets upstairs?" Kristina glanced curiously at the two young guests.

"*Ja, bitte. Danka schoen.*" Mrs. Brown watched as the *frau* bustled from the kitchen. Then, "Joan, Kiki, I'll put in a call to General Brown, see if his office knows anything about where your mother went."

"Why can't we go home?" Joan sounded tired. She leaned away from Kiki, grumbling, "Our dad will have a fit when he hears what Kiki's been up to today."

When everyone started talking at once, Kiki raised her hand. "Mrs. Brown, I'm worried. Mama wouldn't leave a new *fraulien* alone at our house, would she?"

After a minute of silence broken only by a gentle canine snore. Mrs. Brown said quietly, "When you left for school today, did your mother say she'd be going out?"

The girls shook their heads. "The only thing I heard was that Ilse's gone, and we're getting someone new. Someone named Gisela." Joan hesitated. "Mama was running the carpet sweeper when we left. In her bathrobe."

"That was her name, the maid who was there when I got home. Gisela." Kiki frowned. "She was **so** mean."

"You must have felt awful, honey." Mrs. Brown leaned against the sink board. "I think we're worrying about nothing. "You showed up while your mother was out on an errand, Kiki. The new maid didn't know what to do with you. She'll be nicer next time you see her." She smiled at the four teen-agers. "I'll make some calls, find out what I can. Then we'll head over to *Vi erstrasse* and meet this Gisela."

Kiki slumped miserably on the bench. She didn't want to go home. Mama wasn't there, and that terrible *fraulein* was. *Should I tell them Gisela is friends with that awful man?*

No one spoke until Mrs. Brown left the kitchen. Then, quietly, Joan said, "Did Gisela say how Roland got out?"

Kiki shook her head. "No. She was scared of him. You should have heard how he growled when he saw her!" Under the table, Roland pushed his nose into Kiki's hand.

"So, how'd you and Roland meet up with Mom? Were you on the way back to school?" Harold talked through a mouthful of crackers.

"That's right." Joan looked thoughtful. "Why'd you leave the house? You could have just gone upstairs if you wanted to get away from Gisela."

Kiki flashed on the image of Roland halfway out of her parents' bedroom window. "We did go upstairs. Looking out the window—into the back yard, you know? I saw ..." Kiki gagged on a piece of cracker, coughed and continued, "I saw the man who tried to kidnap me. He was on our back porch. Gisela let him come inside."

The air in the Browns' kitchen got very still. Then, Joan whispered, "How can you be sure? It was night; there was a bag over your head."

"I'm positive." Kiki nodded vehemently. "I recognized his voice. It was him."

"Our Mom needs to hear this." Peggy sounded impressed. "Your new maid is friends with him? Ewww!"

"So, you're upstairs and this guy comes into the house? Jeez, Kiki!" Harold dropped the last cracker back on the plate. "What did you do?"

Kiki sighed. *I'm going to have to tell them the truth.* "We— Roland and me—we climbed down a tree outside my parents' bedroom window."

"Holy Cow! Is that *hund* part cat?" Harold burst out laughing.

The older girls both stared at Kiki. Peggy looked impressed; Joan looked dismayed. Finally, Joan whispered, "You went into Mama and Daddy's room?"

"Please don't tell, Joan. I'll never do it again. I had to get out of there."

Joan exhaled. "This has been quite a day, even for you, Sis. First you have a fit in class, then you ditch school, then you go into our parents' bedroom and climb out their window? When Mama and Daddy hear about this, you'll be lucky if they don't send you to Siberia."

Peggy stood, started to leave the kitchen and turned back. "Give her a little slack, Joan. This isn't her fault. She's just a kid." As she left the room, she called, "Mom! You still on the phone?"

Joan's eyebrows went up. She glared at Kiki. "See what you did? Are you satisfied? Peggy's mad at me now." She flounced from the kitchen.

"Whoa! With a sister like that, who needs enemies?" Harold reached out, brushed Kiki's hand with his own and then quickly withdrew it. "You think that new maid and her friend know what's in the shed?" His whisper was barely audible.

"I don't know." Kiki felt bone-tired. "I'm sorry I snapped at you, Harold. Can we be friends again? I'll try to keep my temper."

Harold ran a hand across his chin. "Maybe. I'll think about it." He smiled mischievously. "But only if you tell me what made you ditch school."

CHAPTER NINETEEN

"I'd like to hear that story, too." Mrs. Brown stood in the doorway. She wasn't smiling.

Kiki groaned. Harold's glance went from her to his mother. "It's not a story, Mom. This kid is a little weird but she doesn't lie." He looked somberly up at Mrs. Brown. "What'd you find out?"

Mrs. Brown slipped onto the bench next to her son and folded her hands. "Did I miss the ceremony where your father put you in charge in his absence, Harold?"

Oh, boy. Harold's in for it now. Kiki gulped. "He's just trying to protect me, Mrs. Brown. Nobody, I mean *nobody,* believes me about a bunch of things. Everyone thinks I make up stories to get attention." Kiki's mouth twisted in what she hoped was a smile. She felt like crying. "Everyone but my dad."

"It's true, Mom." Harold jerked a thumb toward Kiki. "This kid has the worst luck ever."

Kiki cringed. *Will she believe us?*

Mrs. Brown looked from her son to the nervous young girl next to him. Her wary expression slowly dissolved into a crinkly smile. "Looks like you two aren't fighting any more. Good." She shook her charm bracelet; the Menorah jingled between a tiny tank and a miniature Statue of Liberty. "My intuition," she glanced at Kiki, "says this little candlestick is at the heart of your troubles. Am I right?"

"Sort of." Kiki hesitated. "Things started going downhill after I found it." She looked anxiously at Harold's mother.

Harold leaned forward. "Mom? Did you find out where Mrs. Moore went? The new *fraulien* at Kiki's house is scary."

Kiki nodded. "If Mama knew Gisela better, she wouldn't have left her in charge."

Mrs. Brown put her hands together in a steeple. "HQ put me on hold, and your mom's friend Doris didn't know anything. Was the Jeep in your driveway? Maybe your mother went to the commissary."

"The Jeep was there." A *frisson* of fear trickled along Kiki's spine.

"*Frau* Brown?" The maid, Kristina, stood in the doorway. "*Ich bin* changing *die bettwasche?*" Shall I change the bed linen?

"*Jah.* I'll help." Mrs. Brown gave the teen-agers an apologetic smile and followed Kristina from the kitchen. As they went up the stairs she said, "Do you know the Moores' new *fraulein*, Gisela?"

"Gisela? *Jah. Ist schwarzmarkt.*" Black Market.

Mrs. Brown stopped in the middle of the stairway. "*Ach.* There's our answer, kids. If Colonel Moore got her through the Black Market, there's no information on her."

"Daddy gets a lot of stuff that way," Kiki spoke up. "I bet he got Ilse there, too. Is that bad?"

"*Der Schwarzhandel ist verboten.*" Kristina's voice was little more than a whisper.

"It's against regulations." Mrs. Brown nodded. "It's faster, though, than going through HQ."

"Maybe Daddy didn't know about regulations." Kiki felt her face getting red. *Are they saying Daddy broke the law?*

"Let's not get sidetracked." Mrs. Brown smiled at Kiki. "Where a *fraulien* came from is not our business. Finish your snack, kids. We're taking Kiki and Joan home." She looked up at Kristina. "Come with us, *bitte*; the sheets can wait. I may need your help talking to Gisela."

Joan and Peggy appeared on the upstairs landing. "Everyone knows why she ditched school today." Joan's voice carried clearly to the kitchen. "She went into a trance or something— did you know she does that, Mrs. Brown? And then she fainted. She'll do anything for attention."

The kitchen became absolutely still. Kiki put her hands over her face and closed her eyes. *If only I could disappear.*

After a long minute, Harold cleared his throat. "You want to tell us what that trance was about, Kiki? You're the last person I'd accuse of seeking attention."

Kiki felt a cool, soft hand covering hers on the table. She looked up into Mrs. Brown's concerned face. "Whatever happened, I don't believe you did it on purpose. Or willingly. Would it help to talk about it?" Mrs. Brown paused. "According to the records I researched, the complex where you're attending school was used as a workhouse during the war. Women and children were drafted into service there to package food and supplies for the *Wermacht*." She looked around the table. "Has your teacher mentioned that?" Harold shook his head. Peggy and Joan just looked guiltily at her.

Mrs. Brown continued, "When people are angry, afraid, terrified, or in extreme pain, the energy from those feelings fills the space around them. It hangs around long after the people have left and can be felt—sometimes, even, seen—by sensitive people." She smiled gently. "Kiki, do you remember anything about what Joan called your 'trance?'"

"There were awful sounds--sirens, booms, screaming." Kiki looked hesitantly at Mrs. Brown. "The building sort of shuddered. Then it tilted, like a boat on water. There was smoke everywhere; I couldn't breathe." She clenched her hands together. "Next thing I knew, all that was gone. I was sitting at the table and everyone was staring at me." She covered her eyes again. *Just like now, except that this time, maybe, someone understands. Is it possible I'm not crazy? Does someone else in the world, besides Daddy and me, see ghosts?*

Joan's voice, high-pitched and tense, cut through the silence. "Shame on you, Kiki, letting other people know how crazy you are! The rest of our family," she looked around the table, "isn't like that; we're normal." Joan glared at her sister.

Kiki lifted her head, ready to run from the kitchen and out of the Browns' house. Joan's outburst, though, had not had the expected effect. Everyone looked really uncomfortable, as if they felt sorry for both of the Moore girls.

Harold finally spoke. "Personally," he turned to Joan, "I'm blown away by your sister's whatchacallit, talent. I just wish she'd let someone help her. Being friends with Kiki is like trying to pet a bobcat."

An awkward laugh erupted around the table. After a minute Peggy said, "I can understand where Joan's coming from, too. It's not easy being the oldest. I'll testify to that."

"*Jah,*" Mrs. Brown said brusquely. "Each of us makes the best of the hand we're dealt." She looked from Harold to Peggy. "The Jeep's not big enough for six. You two, head upstairs to your homework. Kristina and I will take Roland and the girls home."

"But, Mom ..." Harold started. After a glance at his mother, he followed Peggy from the kitchen. At the stairs, though, he looked back at Kiki. "What about the shed?"

"What about it?" Mrs. Brown stopped herding people from

the kitchen. She turned, one arm in her coat sleeve. "Is there something I'm missing?"

Oh, no. Why did I tell Harold about the skeleton? Daddy will be furious! Kiki glared at Harold. "It's just, well, that's where the man grabbed me. Daddy told me not to go in there. He said he'd take care of it when he gets back." She put an anxious hand on Roland's collar.

"I'll make sure your mother knows there's a connection between your new maid and that man." Mrs. Brown took her purse from the boar's head coat rack. "Coming, Kristina?"

The five-minute ride from the Browns' to *Vierstrasse* was awkward: Kiki and Joan hugged opposite sides of the back seat, ignoring each other, Kristina sat nervously in the passenger seat and Mrs. Brown drove silently through the quiet, snow-covered streets.

"There's our Jeep," Kiki pointed to the snow-covered vehicle in the driveway. "It hasn't moved all day."

"Wherever your mother went, she didn't drive." Mrs. Brown glanced at the girls in the rearview mirror. "If she's here, Kristina and I don't need to come in. We can talk to her—tell her what happened to Kiki—on the porch. Otherwise, we'll go in and talk to ... Gisela, is it?"

"Yes, ma'am." Joan sounded unusually subdued. "I hope Mama's there and this is all just one of Kiki's weird dreams."

Kiki shrunk farther into the folds of her hooded jacket. *Weird dreams? You bet. More like a nightmare.* Her lips moved in a silent prayer. *God, please let Mama be at the house. And don't let any more bad stuff happen.*

"Ditto. I'm sure we all agree on that." Mrs. Brown's tone was brusque. "Kristina, tell me honestly: do you think the girls are safe with this Gisela woman if their mother is away?"

Kristina opened the Jeep door and climbed out before answering. "Gisela cleans the *haus,* that's all, *Jah?* Should be safe."

"*Jah, Jah.*" Mrs. Brown muttered. "I hope it's as simple as that."

Joan had one foot on the ground when Roland pushed past her, barking furiously as he bounded across the yard. "Roland! *Stoppen!*" she shouted.

"I'll get him." Kiki hurried around the Jeep. "Roland! Halt!" He turned his head, spittle flying from his jaws. "Sit!" she repeated. He lowered his rear to the stone step, looking back anxiously at the front door. "Good boy!" Kiki picked up the trailing leash and knelt next to him. "Easy, boy," she whispered. "We'll take it from here."

Gisela opened the door, holding a long wooden walking stick. "*Vas is los?*" What's going on?

"*Wo bist Frau* Moore?" Mrs. Brown's voice was calm, authoritative.

"*Ich bin Gisela, der wirtschafter*—the housekeeper." Gisela kept her eyes on Roland; he was on his feet now, growling.

"*Wo bist Muter?*" Joan's voice rose in a nervous squeak.

"*Ausweg.* Out. Frau Moore *bist* out. The *jung frauleins* go in *der haus.*" Gisela eyed Roland and came down the steps. He growled, low in his throat. She retreated. "*Der hund ist verboten.*"

Kristina stepped forward. "Gisela Schmidt? *Ist dein muter* Angeline Schmidt? *Ich bin dein nachbarin*—I'm your neighbor —Kristina Groening." She smiled, holding out a hand.

"Kristina?" Gisela looked uncomfortable. She began talking rapidly in German. Kiki caught the words 'Colonel, and Frankfurt.'

"*Jah, jah,*" Kristina nodded, then turned to Mrs. Brown. "Colonel Moore came and took Frau Moore to Frankfurt before *die nachbarin*—she indicated Gisela—had her training. She is happy to meet the Moore *kinder,* but not the *hund.*"

Mrs. Brown looked first at Gisela, then at Joan and Kiki. "That does make sense, girls. Officers often get a break during maneuvers. Bad timing, though, with the new maid needing instruction."

"Mrs. Brown?" Joan hesitated. "Could Kristina ask her about the man who attacked Kiki? I don't think Mama would want that man in our house."

Kiki's head swiveled toward Harold's mom. She held her breath. *What will Gisela do when she finds out I saw them?*

Mrs. Brown looked first at Joan, then at Gisela. "Is Mrs. Moore expected back tonight?"

"*Ach, Jah. Ich bin* staying here with the *kinder.*" Gisela grinned.

How good is her English? Does she understand what Joan just said? I need to find out. Without another thought Kiki stepped forward. "I saw your cousin, Ilse, wearing Mama's best coat. I know Mama didn't give it to her. Ilse stole it."

Everyone stared at Kiki. Gisela looked like she'd been slapped. Her face went from white, to pink to beet red. "*Was is los mit du? Dumbkopf!*" She pointed the walking stick at Kiki, then at Joan. "Inside, now, *dumbkopf kinder*! No *essen* t onight!"

It was as if someone had tossed a grenade into the Moore's yard. Roland lunged for Gisela, Kiki grabbed for his leash, Joan ducked behind Mrs. Brown, and Kristina hopped back into the Jeep, cowering. Mrs. Brown stood perfectly still, shouting, "Halt!"

Roland dropped to the ground, muzzle between his paws. Kiki fell to her knees next to him, wincing at leash burns.

"Kristina!" Mrs. Brown's voice boomed.

"*Jah?*" The Browns' maid sounded terrified.

Mrs. Brown lowered her voice. "Tell this, this *fraulien* the Moore *kinder* will be staying with us tonight. She's to have

Frau Moore contact us the minute she returns."

No one said a word.

"And Kiki, get that damn dog in the Jeep, STAT."

CHAPTER TWENTY

Mrs. Brown threw the Jeep into reverse, backed out of the driveway and accelerated hard down the street, jaw set menacingly..

Five minutes passed before she let out an explosive breath. "I have never, in my entire life, heard such insolence! Such downright meanness! That, that sorry excuse for a housekeeper! Your mother ... your father ... the General will hear about this, or my name isn't Sarah Elizabeth Brown." She made eye contact with Joan and Kiki in the rearview mirror. "You girls look scared. Well, you should be. Not of me, though." Her face softened a little. "That Black Market *fraulein* understood every word Kiki said."

"Yes, ma'am," Joan whispered. Kiki opened her mouth, but no words came out.

"Ma'am? Mrs. Brown?" Joan glanced at Kiki, then at the scarf-covered back of Mrs. Brown's head. "If Kiki really saw someone in Mama's coat, what is Mama wearing? It doesn't make sense. She wouldn't leave the house without her coat."

Kiki loosened her grip on Roland—he was still agitated, whining and scratching at the door handle—and blurted, "She didn't take her pocketbook, either. I saw it on the floor next to Mama and Daddy's bed."

"This situation stinks to high heaven." Mrs. Brown glanced at the girls in the rearview mirror, then pulled over and parked the Jeep in a patch of snow. "Okay, girls." She turned to face Kiki and Joan. "Let's review what we know: Your mother was at home this morning when you left for school, right?"

The girls nodded.

"When Kiki went home--around lunchtime, Kiki? She wasn't there."

Again, the girls nodded. Kiki said, "That *fraulien*, Gisela was in the kitchen acting like she owned the place. She told me to leave. From my own house!"

"She said your parents went somewhere together?"

"Yes. She said they're coming back tonight, and she's in charge until then."

"Don't forget about Roland," Joan put in. "Kiki found him wandering a long way from home. How'd he get out? And why'd he run off? He knows he's supposed to guard our house when Daddy's not there."

"That's right." Mrs. Brown tapped the steering wheel with her fingers. "Why, exactly, did you and Roland climb out the upstairs window?" Mrs. Brown turned her piercing brown-eyes on Kiki.

Gulp. "I saw that man--the one who grabbed me--go in the house through the back door. I was scared he would come after me." Kiki shivered, just thinking about it.

Mrs. Brown reached back and patted Kiki's bony knee. "You're a very courageous girl, Kiki Moore." Then, "I'm so glad you had the presence of mind to confront Gisela about your mother's coat. That brought her up short! Add to all of this what Kristina said about those *frauleins* being Black Market, and I'm worried. When you go through proper channels, you get an important layer of legitimacy. Not to mention, an Air Force wife would never leave a stranger in charge of her home ...." She straightened and leaned out the side of the Jeep. "Is that Harold and Peggy down the street?"

Joan and Kiki both turned to look. Two blocks away, bent against the cold and walking fast, they saw the tall, lanky outlines of Harold and Peggy.

"Can I hop out and get them?" Kiki felt a rush of pleasure at the sight of her friends. "Please don't be mad at them for disobeying you, Mrs. Brown. It's only because they're worried about Joan and me."

"Go for it." Mrs. Brown didn't sound mad at all.

Roland must have thought she meant him, too; he pushed past Kiki and plunged from the Jeep, racing along the icy path toward Peggy and Harold.

"Wait for me!" Kiki yelled. *How am I supposed to keep up with a German Shepherd?*

Harold and Peggy stared as the big dog raced toward them. When he skidded to a stop they both dropped to their knees and hugged him, laughing.

"Some welcome, huh?" Kiki bent over, out of breath. "You're lucky he likes you. You should have seen him a little while ago."

"Didn't go so well, huh? That why Mom's taking you back to our house?" Harold got to his feet.

Kiki nodded. "Yeah."

Peggy stood and picked up the end of Roland's leash. "No more questions, little brother." She started up the path. "You know Mom hates waiting."

Mrs. Brown stood leaning against the Jeep, arms folded. Kiki groaned. *She's mad. Will she send us back home?*

"Fall in, troops." At Mrs. Brown's nod Kristina and Joan climbed out and stood next to Peggy, Harold and Kiki.

"Do you want us by height or by age?" Peggy left the middle of the line and went to stand between Harold and Kristina. This put Joan and Kiki at the end. "How's this?"

What's going on? Kiki bent forward to look along the line, trying not to laugh. *We make a sorry bunch of soldiers.* Kristina was dressed in a skirt, pinafore, and babushka; Peggy and Joan wore faux fur parkas and knee boots; and Harold slouched grimly in a long, moth=eaten overcoat and knit cap. "Should Roland be in the line, Mrs. Brown?"

"Jah."

Roland, sitting next to Mrs. Brown, wagged his tail. When Kiki snapped her fingers he went to stand next to her.

"Okay," Mrs. Brown barked. "Attention: For the ride home, Kristina, you're in front; Joan, Kiki and Roland, back seat; Peggy and Harold—this is the chance you've been waiting for. Do not, I said DO NOT, tell the General—you'll stand on the running board on either side, holding on tight." Mrs. Brown got into the driver's seat and started the engine. "God help us if we pass any MPs on the way."

Kristina, Joan, Kiki and Roland piled in, then Peggy and Harold climbed onto the running boards on either side of the vehicle. Peggy shouted, "Ready to roll, Mom!"

"Who knew Mrs. Brown could be so much fun?" Joan whispered into Kiki's ear. Kiki nodded. *If we're Mrs. Brown's soldiers, I like this army.*

When they pulled into the driveway at the Browns' house, Mrs. Brown barked, "Conference in the kitchen in five minutes, sharp!"

"Ten-hup!" Four teen-aged voices shouted.

Peggy opened the front door to the sharp **Ring! Ring!** of the phone.

Kristina dashed into the kitchen, muttering, *"Eine minute, bitte."* She answered, then handed the receiver to Mrs. Brown.

"Danke. Maybe it's HQ." Mrs. Brown turned Peggy toward the living room before speaking into the receiver.

With a finger to her lips for silence, Peggy herded everyone to the comfortable-looking plush couch and club chairs. Kiki sank down onto the couch and closed her eyes. *Please God, let that be HQ saying Mama's okay.*

Five minutes later by the Roman numerals on the Browns' mantle clock, Mrs. Brown came through the kitchen's swinging door. There was an odd, almost scared look on her face. Everyone stopped talking—Joan in mid-sentence—and stared at her. Mrs. Brown spoke to Kristina first: "The sheet-changing can wait. Stay with us, please. I need to have a word with you and the *kinder.*"

"Jah, jah. Danke Schoen." Kristina stood awkwardly near the stairs.

Mrs. Brown gave Joan and Kiki the briefest of smiles. "These are the facts as we know them: Emily Moore was home when the girls left for school. She was not there when Kiki arrived home around lunchtime; The new *fraulein* said she was with her husband. That call just now? HQ: Colonel Moore is still on maneuvers and has not been given leave to come home."

Joan and Kiki looked at each other. Joan mouthed, "Where is Mama?" Kiki gulped and shook her head.

"Add to this," Mrs. Brown continued, "the new *fraulien's* reaction when Kiki mentioned seeing someone wearing her mother's coat. I'm worried."

"Should we call the MPs, Mom?" Peggy's face paled. "Maybe the same person who tried to snatch Kiki, got Mrs. Moore."

Peggy's words hung in the air. Then everyone began

talking.

"We tried that. They won't help." Joan groaned.

"What else can we do?" from Harold.

"There's more," Kiki whispered. The room got quiet. "Mama's pocketbook, remember? I saw it on the floor next to her bed."

"Maybe it was an extra pocketbook." Mrs. Brown looked thoughtful. "She probably has more than one."

"It's time to tell what you found in the shed, Kiki." Harold glanced at her, then looked away.

"*Ach du Lieber gott!*" Kristina put her hands up to her face. "*Das Gerucht*, the stories, they are true?"

"What stories, Kristina?" Mrs. Brown's voice was quiet, but commanding. "Tell us."

"About that *haus. Ich bin* thinking it is *das marchen*--fairy tales--but now? Maybe not." She cleared her throat. "The family who live there? People say they hide treasures and help Jews escape. When they *verschwinden*—disappear, stories stop." She added quietly, "So many stories just like theirs. My heart hurts for them." She looked down at her feet and whispered, "and for *Das Vaterland.*"

"That house, with its background, was commandeered for American dependents? Shameful!" Two bright red spots appeared on Mrs. Brown's cheeks. "Harold, what has Kiki not told us about the shed? Speak up, young man."

Harold shook his head and turned to Kristina. "Who was in that family? What were *das marchen*, the tales, about them?"

"They were *die Strassburgs. Herr Strassburg's* shop still carries his name on *der* window." Kristina ran her hand across her face again. "*Herr und Frau Strassburg habe ein tochter,* daughter, *mit ein kinder.*" A little boy.

.

"Harold ...." Mrs. Brown's tone was flat, menacing.

He looked nervously at his mother, but continued, "What

kind of shop, Kristina?"

"*Juwelen*--Jewelry." Kristina hardly breathed the word. Then, half to herself, *alles verloren ist*--everything was lost."

"Perhaps not." Mrs. Brown perched on an arm of the couch, looking slightly more relaxed. "That could explain the attack on Kiki. Maybe someone thinks the *Strassburgs* hid their store goods—jewelry—in the bomb shelter."

Joan cleared her throat. "This is interesting--at least to Kiki, maybe—but it doesn't get us any closer to finding Mama." She glared at her sister. "Are you sure she wasn't there earlier? Maybe you just didn't notice. Your nickname's not Looney Tunes for nothing."

Everyone looked at Kiki. She slumped back against the fuzzy cushions, frowning. "I did notice," she whispered. "Mama wasn't there. And, your question about the shed, Mrs. Brown?"

"Yes, Kiki?" Mrs. Brown gave Joan and Harold both withering glances. "I'm listening."

"There was a trapdoor going down to the bomb shelter. Except, it wasn't. A bomb shelter, I mean. It was a storage room. And I saw a very small, very real skeleton down there, lying on a cot."

"Oh, boy," Peggy breathed. "How awful, Kiki."

Joan wrinkled her nose. "Don't waste your sympathy, Peggy. She's always finding repulsive stuff. It's like she's a gross-magnet."

"That's quite enough, Joan." Mrs. Brown's tone was brusque. "I think the General will be interested in that cellar. I'll put in a call to him right now." She went back into the kitchen.

Peggy looked from Joan to Kiki to Harold. "We're a pretty sorry-looking crew.. Let's take a break while Mom's on the phone. Want to work on our homework, Joan? Go over the chapter for tomorrow's science test?" She headed for the stairs.

"Sure. Anything to quit talking about skeletons." Joan

scowled at her sister and followed Peggy up the stairs.

Harold was quiet for a minute after the older girls left. Finally, without looking at Kiki he said, "Sorry for pressuring you into telling."

"It's okay. It's not your fault my sister is so mean. She's right, though. I am the family screw-up." Kiki sighed. "I wish I could make that Gisela person tell us where Mama is."

"That makes two of us, Kiki." Mrs. Brown stood in the doorway. "The General's not in his office, but I spoke to his secretary. Turns out a certain element has been trying to take over your property," she glanced at Kiki, "for some time. It looks like your father played right into their hands when he got house help through the Black Market."

"What's so special about our house?" As Kiki said it, she knew the answer: the shed and what was beneath it. She thought of the little boy ghost. *Oh, no. I bet he's part of this mess, poor thing!*

Harold smiled. "You asking, or just thinking out loud?"

Mrs. Brown chuckled softly. "Kiki has a higher opinion of your intelligence than you do, Harold." She studied the young girl across the table. Are you still worried about your mom? Because I certainly am."

CHAPTER TWENTY-ONE

"Yes, ma'am." Kiki looked down at her chipped, bitten fingernails. "I appreciate your help, Mrs. Brown. I keep wondering if Mama's hurt, or …." Kiki couldn't finish.

"Don't jump to conclusions, honey." Mrs. Brown stood and left the room, muttering, "I hope this teaches Colonel Moore a lesson. Dealing in the Black Market and putting his family at risk like this? Shameful."

Her soft-spoken words resounded in the quiet kitchen. Harold glanced at Kiki and got to his feet "Let's get out of here."

Kiki sank back into the cushions, turning away so he couldn't see her tears. "To go where?" she muttered. "I'm through wandering around in the cold."

Harold snapped his fingers at Roland. "C'mon, boy! Kiki, put your coat on."

A minute later, shivering on the front steps while Roland

lifted his leg against a snow-covered bush, Harold talked to the air space next to Kiki's head. "Mom didn't really mean it. She gets weird like that when she's worried."

Kiki looked past Harold to the cobblestone street, where snow-packed crevices formed a muddy cross-work pattern. "My dad is **not** shameful. He would never purposely do anything to hurt us. He wouldn't. He loves us." She stamped her foot in frustration. "Doesn't your mom know that?"

Harold jammed his fists in his pockets. After a minute he ventured, "Don't take it personally. My mom is used to fixing problems—it's a military-wife thing—and she can't fix this one."

The anger leaked out of Kiki, leaving her weak and hopeless. She sat down on the bottom step, hugging her knees. "It **is** personal, Harold. Daddy did what he always does. He tried to cut corners. Now Mama's missing and Joan and I can't go home." She looked up at Harold. "The MPs won't help us; your mom tried but she can't; I KNOW something's fishy at our house." She got to her feet. "I'm going back over there. I have to find my mother."

Harold glanced back at the front door. "I'll come with you. We have to clear it with my mom, though. I'll catch hell, otherwise."

Kiki sighed. "Go back inside. There's no point asking for permission; she'll just say no." She picked up Roland's leash and left the yard.

"Wait." Harold's call, as he turned to go back in the house, sounded half-hearted.

Kiki walked faster, then broke into a run. Roland loped along next to her, stretching his legs enthusiastically. "You get it, don't you, boy?" She lengthened her stride to keep up with him. "We have a job to do. Let's do it."

When the Browns' house was out of sight Kiki slowed to a walk.

I need to make a plan. Let's see: I can't let Gisela know I'm back. Maybe I'll stay outside and look for clues. Mama's probably not in the house, anyway. I would have seen her when I got home from school. I should keep my eyes open. If they took Mama away against her will, maybe she dropped a clue, a hankie or something.

Roland stiffened, ears forward and head down. Farther along the snow-speckled path Kiki saw an old, hunched over woman— 'crones,' Daddy called them—walking with a small child.

"At ease, boy." Kiki pulled him off the path and into the road. "We'll cross the street, give them lots of room. Be nice, boy." She bent and patted Roland's head. "The only enemy we have right now is Gisela. Let's keep it that way." When she looked up, the woman's arms were wrapped around the child. It was a boy, judging from the baggy coveralls. The woman stared grimly at the *Americaner* with the war *hund.*

Kiki kept herding Roland toward the other side of the street. After a silent minute—Roland's panting and the squish of her feet in the mud didn't count—she heard a raspy, *"Guten tag, fraulein!"* followed by a second, lisping, *"Guten tag!"*

Kiki turned, waved to them and called back, *Guten tag!"*

When they reached the far side of the street they watched the *frau* and her *kinder* round the corner. "Good boy," Kiki whispered to Roland. "We need all the friends we can get."

At the corner of *Vierstrasse* Kiki decided to seek cover like the WWII soldiers she'd seen in movie newsreels. She wrapped her fingers around Roland's collar, crouched down and crab-walked from one overgrown cedar bush to the next. Roland caught on fast, nudging Kiki forward with his nose.

Vierstrasse was, as usual, quiet. A short, upsloping street, there was a big, Tyrolean-style mansion at one end and modest homes on each side. The Moores' house, fourth on the left, was separated from the mansion property by a dense, ancient hedge.

When Kiki and Roland reached the Moores' yard she signaled 'Stay' and pulled apart scratchy, fragrant cedar branches to reconnoiter.

At first glance the house looked benign. Curtains were drawn in the two upstairs windows; the long rays of late afternoon sun reflected off them. *Mama doesn't usually close those curtains until nighttime.*

Smoke drifted lazily from the back chimney.. *Someone's in the kitchen. Maybe not, though. Mama keeps that fire banked to keep the embers alive.*

The Jeep hadn't moved. Now completely covered with snow, it reminded Kiki of a giant, misshapen marshmallow. The thought made her stomach growl. She giggled and looked toward the back yard. *Doggone it! I can't see anything but that one corner. Doesn't look like anyone's back there.*

On the ground next to the Jeep, clear as anything in the layered snow, Kiki saw large, deep footprints. *In case anyone thinks I imagined that man going into our kitchen. Unless he stepped in the same footprints coming out, he's still here.*

For a second Kiki was back at the door of the shed. rough arms gripping her and a scratchy, stinky cloth pressed against her face. She shook herself. *Get a grip! I'm useless if I panic.* Her mouth twitched in a grimace. *I'll let myself panic after I know Mama's safe.*

By taking giant steps Kiki placed her feet in the already-made impressions. She looked back, saw Roland's fresh prints next to the older ones, and shrugged. *Oh, well; I tried.*

Roland, already at the far corner of the house, looked back at Kiki. She mouthed, 'Halt.' When she reached him, she gave him a quick pat and looked around the yard. The shed's weathered walls stood, alone and isolated, beyond snow-speckled ground and leafless bushes.

Kiki took a step into the yard, just far enough to see that the kitchen door was closed. A ribbon of light gleamed from a gap in the window curtains.

They're in there. In our kitchen. Please, God, let Mama be somewhere else—shopping or something. Anywhere but here.

Kiki crept to the steps, pretending she was a Tinkerbell fairy floating a few inches off the ground. Roland moved as if he was stalking prey—stealthy, ominous.

Should I peek in the keyhole, or listen at the door? Neither; someone might catch me. Kiki shivered. *I'll climb up and look in the window. If I see Mama, I'll knock on the door and this whole thing will be over.*

At that heartening thought. Kiki leaned over the porch railing and squinted in through the gap between the window frame and the curtain. Her view—one side of the kitchen table, a patch of linoleum floor and the door to the foyer—revealed nothing. *Where is everyone?* Suddenly Gisela spoke, sounding as if she was right next to Kiki. "*Gott in Himmel, du bist eine dumbkopf! Verlassen!* I don't need you!"

Good grief, she's on the other side of this wall!

A man's voice cut across Gisela's. "*Nein, Nein! Ich werde dich nicht verlassen damit du den Schatz nimmst!*"

Kiki groaned, wishing she understood more German. *Are they arguing about Mama? About Joan and me?*

Kiki slumped against the shingled wall, thinking hard. When Roland pushed his nose against her ear she whispered, "Got any ideas, boy?" Roland looked at her, then turned and trotted across the yard to the shed. He sniffed below the door and began digging.

What if they look out the window? They'll see him. Kiki dashed across the yard and grabbed Roland's collar, hissing, "Stop! Halt! They'll catch us!" He tilted his head and looked at her, one muddy paw raised, then went back to digging.

He won't stop. She looked up at the handle; the lock dangled uselessly by one loop. *Why isn't it locked? I'll think about that later.* She opened the door, just a crack. Roland immediately pushed his shoulders through and disappeared into the dark interior. *Here goes nothing.* Kiki slipped in after him.

She stood still, waiting for her eyes to adjust. She felt Roland's fur against her leg, heard him panting. The quietest of growls rumbled from his throat. She looked down, ready to reassure him, and choked back a scream. There, perched on top of the crate—it was still in place over the cellar door—sat the little boy ghost. He looked up at her, scowling.

Kiki remembered to breathe through the fear enveloping her. She said, as calmly as she could, "Have you seen the *frau* who lives here? *Mein mutter?*"

The small figure, hardly more than a wisp of smoke, slid from the trunk and hovered next to it. Kiki relaxed. He was so tiny, so transparent.

A breeze brushed Kiki's cheek; she thought she heard a whispered, *"Du bist Nazi?"*

"No. *Nein.* I'm not a *Nazi.*" She shook her head. "I'm an American. *Americaner.*" Frustrated tears filled her eyes. She shook them away. Roland, next to her, whined softly. *He's not growling any more. He can see the ghost, or at least feel its presence.*

"Please help me, little boy." Kiki spoke softly. *I wonder if he knows he's dead.*

The wispy figure reached out and touched Roland's ear. The ear twitched.

Outside, the kitchen door opened. Voices drifted out; snatches of a conversation moved toward the shed.

They're coming! It's dark in here. Maybe they won't see us. No. They'll have a light. Where can we go? Into the cellar. Kiki wrenched the crate up, urged Roland into the yawning hole and climbed in after him.

Roland scrambled down the ladder without a sound. Kiki, on his tail, missed a ladder rung and fell the last three feet. She landed face-down on the cellar's dirt floor.

"Oof! Sorry, boy." She rolled away from Roland, peering into the darkness. *I wish I had night vision, like bats. Oh, no! Are there bats down here?* She swept the air in a circle with her hands, hoping to feel what she couldn't see. Her fingers brushed Roland's damp nose. His response, a quick tongue-licking, reassured her.

Gradually the space—a twenty-foot square, low-ceilinged room—became dimly visible. "See those cots over there, Roland? Don't go over there. *Nein.* There's a skeleton on one of them." Roland, moving slowly toward the cots, turned around and came back to Kiki.

"Do you think they stashed Mama down here?" Kiki pushed the awful thought away and looked around, squinting for details through the gloom.

The cots took up one wall, shelves lined another, and a table occupied a third. *That looks like a kerosene lantern on the table. I wish I could light it.*

The fourth wall, behind the ladder, was in complete darkness. Kiki took a few steps. *This must be what it's like to be blind.* When her outstretched hand bumped the ladder, she stopped. *I'll wait. Maybe my eyes will adjust.* Gradually, the wall behind the ladder took shape. She could make out four wooden knobs spaced evenly half-way up the wall. *Cupboards. Storage cupboards.*

"*Das ist verboten!*"

The words tickled Kiki's ear like an angry mosquito. She froze, so terrified she stopped breathing. "What? Who's here?" She felt Roland's fur against her leg and leaned down, grabbing his collar. "Did you hear something, boy?"

A shiver ran down Kiki's spine. She forced herself to relax, focusing on the cupboards. "What would anyone store down here? Potatoes, maybe." She touched one of the knobs. Immediately, her fingers turned icy cold. "Eek!" She yanked her hand back and took a step away. *What's going on?*

"Verboten!" Louder this time, and hissed menacingly.

Roland snapped at the air and growled.

Another ghost? The thought was too much for Kiki. She dropped to the floor, terrified.

"Owoo, Owoo!" Roland's anxious howl broke through Kiki's terror. She slipped an arm around his neck. "Shh! They'll hear you!"

"Weggehen meine fader's gelt!" The little boy ghost appeared inches from Kiki's head, glowing an angry red.

"What? *Ich verstehen nicht."* I don't understand.

The ghost drifted over to the cupboards. A line of wavy red sparks appeared across the wall. *"Verboten!"*

As Kiki sat there, stunned, the ghost stuck his tongue out at her and faded away.

Silence settled over the dark cellar. The ghost's words flashed across Kiki's brain. *Gelt? That's the word for gold. Fader means father. Weggehen? Whatever that means, it's not good.* She squinted at the cupboards. *Why doesn't he want me to look in there?"*

She stood and moved toward the cupboard wall, expecting any minute to be assaulted. She reached out, grasped one of the knobs, and pulled. With an alarmingly loud **Creak,** the door opened. Kiki could just make out, within the cupboard's recesses, stacks of small boxes and cloth-wrapped objects.

Potatoes? A nervous giggle erupted from her lips. She pulled at one of the cloths. It fell away, revealing something pale yellow and flat. *Definitely not potatoes.* She took a breath and stretched her fingers toward the object.

It was cold. smooth, and bordered with what felt like sharp pebbles. Kiki's stomach flip-flopped. *Metal. And rocks.* She pulled her hand back, closed the cupboard and stepped back, feeling light-headed. *I think I just touched gold and jewels.* Cold sweat trickled down the back of her neck. "We need to get out of here, puppy. On the double!"

Roland moved toward the ladder. "That's right. Good boy." She grabbed his forelegs and boosted him onto the lowest rung.

Heavy footsteps sounded above them.

Someone's in the shed! Are they coming down here? Holy cow!

Kiki dropped off the ladder, pulling Roland down, too. As she crouched on the cellar floor she muttered, "God, please don't let them catch us. I promise I'll be so good from now on, you won't even know it's me." As an afterthought, she made the sign of the cross on her chest. She wasn't Catholic, but maybe God was.

The sound of footsteps mixed with murmuring voices, one deep and rumbling, one shrill. Suddenly, someone screamed. Then, **thump!** Something fell. Roland scrambled to his feet, looking up the ladder and whining.

Could that be Mama? Have they hurt Mama?

There were shuffling sounds, and muted voices. Kiki heard the shed's outer door open and shut. Then, silence. Deadly silence.

Panic took over. Without thinking, Kiki scrambled up the ladder and pushed the trapdoor open. Roland lunged past her and onto the shed floor, snarling.

"Mama? Mama?"

The shed was empty. Kiki climbed out and dropped to the floor, shaky with relief. *Mama's not here. Maybe that wasn't her screaming.*

As she looked around, feeling oddly vulnerable above ground, Kiki muttered, "We have to get out of here." This was followed by, "I'm talking to myself." She smiled. Daddy used to make jokes about his mother, the grandmother Kiki had never met. He said she talked to herself. *Guess it runs in the family.*

She opened the shed door, looked out, then quickly closed it. *I didn't see anyone. Doesn't mean they're not out there.* She wondered who had screamed, then thought of her gentle, lovely mother. *They wouldn't hurt her, would they? They'd have no reason to. They had no reason to hurt me, though, and they did.*

Kiki looked down at Roland. "Here's the plan: We sneak around the house to the climbing tree. You hide in the bushes. I climb up, go in the window, and find Mama."

CHAPTER TWENTY-TWO

The back yard on this late afternoon still had that empty feeling. *Doesn't mean they aren't watching from one of the windows.* Kiki choked back acrid, panic-induced bile while Joan's voice echoed in her brain: 'A thirteen-year-old girl, trying to outsmart criminals? Get a clue!'

These people may be murderers. They may have killed that child. They'll do anything to get that treasure. Is Mama already dead? Kiki clenched her teeth. *She can't be. I have to find her.*

She looked down at Roland. He lay next to her, head resting on his paws. "Let's go, boy. Stay behind me."

She ran around to the bedroom side of the house, imagining herself as blending in first with the shed's weathered siding, then with the dead-looking shrubbery along the fence. "Made it!" She slid in to 'home base,' the rhododendron bush under her parents' bedroom window. Roland bumped her gently as he slid to a stop. "You okay?" Kiki nuzzled the German Shepherd's fur.

"He is. How about you?"

For a second, Kiki stopped breathing. Her eyes went to the jeans-clad legs on the other side of Roland, then up to the bomber-jacket, brown scarf and weather-chapped teen face. "Harold?" came out in an embarrassing squeak.

"It's not Santa Claus." Harold pulled Kiki to her feet.

"What are you doing here? I mean, gosh, am I glad to see you."

Harold gave Roland a quick pat. "Found your mom yet?"

"Nope. Your mom know you're here?"

Harold nodded, then jerked a thumb toward the property next door.

Right. Better to talk over there. "Follow me." Kiki darted across the grass to the brick wall at the property line. She had paused, one leg over the wall, when Roland vaulted past her and landed gracefully on the other side.

"Hubba, Hubba!" Harold hissed. He put a hand on Kiki's back and pushed, then swung his legs up and over. They landed feet first in a pile of dirty snow.

A minute later, huddled on a rusting wrought-iron bench that couldn't be seen from the Moore's house, Harold gave Kiki a crooked grin. "You okay? Still in one piece? Still ornery?" Before she could answer, he added, "My mom went nuts when she found out you took off. First time I ever saw her so worried she forgot to be mad."

She didn't come with you, though. She's probably washed her hands of this mess. Kiki groaned. "It's just ..." she began.

"I know. You think no one else gets it that your mom is in danger." Harold shook his head. "You're wrong."

Should I tell him about the jewels? Will he believe me? This isn't the movies or a story book. This is real life. I wouldn't believe it if I hadn't seen them. She sighed. *I'd better keep it a secret for now.* "I have to get back in the house, Harold. And, somehow, I have to get my dad to come home."

Harold looked up at her, eyes narrowed. "Have you entirely lost it? Those are both terrible ideas. What's going on under that frizz you call a hairdo?"

Kiki straightened, instantly angry. She took a breath and made herself relax. *Don't get mad. So, he got his manners out of a Crackerjack box; at least he's here and wants to help.*

She gazed around the neighbor's expansive, carefully landscaped estate grounds. A row of rose bushes, bare of leaves but still thorny, formed a natural barrier between the curved driveway and the peak-roofed mansion. Suddenly Daddy's frowning face, bushy eyebrows tilted above piercing black eyes, appeared in her mind. *Did he know about the treasure, all along? Is that why he moved us here, why he and Ilse were buddies? No. Daddy's not the most honest person, but he loves us. He wouldn't put us in danger on purpose, just for treasure. Would he?* She shook her head, ashamed of the disloyal thoughts. But the damage was done. She felt more alone, more lost than ever in her life.

"I think ..." Kiki chose her words carefully, "I know what they're after, Gisela, that man, and Ilse. We have to find my mom." She shivered. "Whatever else is going on, I know she wouldn't take off somewhere without telling Joan and me."

Harold looked away, apparently memorizing the front of the mansion. "Anyone live in that place?" He spoke so quietly, Kiki wondered if he was thinking out loud.

Following his glance, she studied the solidly built, fortress-like square. The brick-and-stucco front had six windows upstairs, three on the ground floor. All were tightly shuttered. Snow drifts covered the porch steps. "Doesn't look like it. We're not supposed to be on this property. Joan asked, once; Daddy told us to keep our noses out of Germany's business." She shivered. "Whatever that means."

Harold stamped his feet, knocking clumps of snow off his boots. "You said you think you know what that maid of yours is after. Care to share?"

Kiki shook her head. "I have to tell my dad first. Sorry. Let's just concentrate on finding Mama, okay?" She touched the back of Harold's hand with her fingertips, just for a moment.

Harold looked down at his hand and then straightened, crossing his arms against his chest. "Jeez, Kiki, it's not like I'm going to blab your secret to the world. Knowing what those guys are after could help us find your mother." He made a hollow effort to laugh. "Let's get moving; I'm slowly becoming an ice sculpture here."

Kiki nodded, shaky with relief. *He's mad, but he didn't leave.*

They hurried along the mansion's withered lawn to the driveway, where a pair of towering holly bushes stood at the gate. They pushed between shiny, spiked leaves and tiny red berries for a view of the Moores' house.

Why are the living room drapes drawn? It's not even dark yet.

"You have a plan?" Harold's whisper was loud against the silent landscape.

"I was gonna climb in the upstairs window. Since you're here, maybe we could just go to the door and make up an excuse to get inside. You could keep Gisela busy while I run upstairs."

Harold looked directly at Kiki for the first time since they'd left the bench. "I'll tell her you need your school books. I'll distract her—maybe head for the kitchen. You sneak in and run upstairs." He smiled, just for a second.

It's a start.

"What about Roland? What do we do with him?" Kiki looked away so Harold wouldn't see the relief she felt.

Harold looked down at the German Shepherd wedged between them in the holly bush. "He'll stand guard at your escape route—that tree outside your parents' window."

Kiki nodded, stepping out of the foliage.

"One last thing." Harold sounded nervous. "Your mom wasn't around when you were in the house before. Why do you think she's there now?"

The question, such a simple one, shook Kiki. She stuttered, "B-because she has to be. She just has to!" She stopped talking, then whispered, "I didn't look everywhere; I wasn't thinking about Mama, just about myself."

Harold chuckled softly. "You're more normal than you realize, kid. Don't sweat it. Let's figure out where you're going to look; you won't have much time."

"Okay. Let's see: no place downstairs except the hall closet; upstairs, the doors were all open before, so, nowhere. Only place left is ...." Kiki's eyes widened. She looked beyond Harold toward the house, murmuring, "*Mein Kampf.*"

"What? Hitler's book? What about it?"

"Nothing, just keep your eye on the top windows when you're looking for my signal, okay?" Kiki touched Roland's head for good luck and tip-toed up the front steps, pressing herself against the wall between the door and the porch railing.

Harold, close behind, gave Roland a hand signal and the dog disappeared around the corner of the house.

Thank goodness he's so well trained! Kiki grinned. *Roland, not Harold.*

After facing the door and squaring his shoulders, Harold knocked softly. Nothing happened. Kiki listened for footsteps from inside but heard only muted voices.

He knocked again, this time a loud rap. The talking stopped. A few seconds later someone threw the bolt and the door opened an inch.

"*Jah?*" Gisela growled.

"*Ich ... ich bin* here for Kiki's school books. For *Schule,*" Harold stuttered, his voice hoarse.

Kiki cringed. *Can she tell how scared he is?*

"*Kiki? Das kinder? Wo ist sie?*" Gisela opened the door a

little wider.

Harold stuck in a foot and stepped over the threshold. "The books are in the kitchen. In the *kuche*. I'll get them.*"*

The door closed with a snap. Kiki counted thirty seconds, then pushed it open and peeked in. The foyer was empty. Harold stood in the kitchen doorway with his back to her. His arms were spread out so he almost completely blocked the view of the foyer.

Yes! She was across the worn carpet in a flash, climbing the stairs quickly and avoiding the creaky spots. On the landing she looked around. The only closed door was the one leading to the maid's room—the attic. *Why didn't I notice that before? Because it's always closed.*

As she touched the cold brass knob, she had a moment of dismay: *What if it's locked?* When the knob turned easily, another fear crept in: *What if Mama's not up there? Do I have time to look anywhere else?* Voices—Harold's and Gisela's—floated up from the kitchen. She pulled the door open, slipped inside, closed the door behind her. When her foot touched the first step, she remembered the sound of Ilse's tread on this staircase. *We could hear it from our room. That's how we knew where she was.* Kiki willed herself to tread lightly. *Like a ghost.*

With the doors closed top and bottom, the staircase was a stuffy, chimney-like tunnel. Kiki fought back terror at the cloying, almost smothering darkness by focusing on Mama's gentle smile, then trying to remember how many steps there were. Thirteen? Twelve? When her forehead touched wood, she knew she was at the top.

She felt for the doorknob, tried to turn it. Nothing happened. The staircase's top door, the one into the maid's quarters, was locked. Her fingers brushed the outline of an old-fashioned keyhole beneath the knob. *We keep the key in it when no one's using the room. Where's the doggone key?*

She put her ear to the door and whispered, "Mama? Are you

in there?" No response. The darkness seemed to swallow her words.

Kiki dropped onto the top step and leaned against the wall, running her fingers along the door. It had evidently been made for some other doorway; there was a gap of about an inch between the bottom of the door and the threshold. *The maid's quarters got a leftover door—the people who built this house were cheapskates..*

As she studied the gap, her eyes slightly unfocused, its shadows changed slightly. She blinked. *Did I really see that? Maybe the curtains moved in the breeze. No. This room's window doesn't open.*

Kiki bent double on the staircase's top step and peered under the door, her breath dislodging generations of dust as she got a mouse's eye view of the floor beyond.

The room was dark, but not as dark as the stairway. The pull-down blind didn't quite fit the window—no surprise—and light came in from both sides. Kiki couldn't see the window; her view was limited to an edge of the old carpet. By squinting, she saw two shapes. *The bedposts.* She sat back, wiped her eyes on her sleeve, and looked again. This time she added a tremulous, "Mama?"

A foot, white, bare, and with bright red toenails, appeared between the bedposts. The polish was Mama's shade. The quietest of murmurs, really just a butterfly wing of sound, brushed Kiki's ear. "Kiki?"

Shocked almost into panic, Kiki gave herself a firm pinch on the arm. She wanted to scream for Harold, run for help, yell Mama's name as loud as she could. *I have to stay calm. I have to keep my wits about me. I found my Mama. And she's alive. I can't fall apart now.*

On the ground floor below, the front door slammed. *Harold must be outside now. We're in here alone with those people, me and Mama. And something's wrong with her. If they find me, they'll kill us both.* Kiki forced herself to breathe. *I can't think that way. I have to concentrate on getting this door open.*

She got to her feet, explored the lock with her fingers, and remembered something Joan had said once about picking locks with a bobby pin. *Could that work? Joan was smart before she became a teen-ager.*

Kiki pulled the three-inch metal clip from her hair and brushed the resulting mass of frizz back from her forehead. *Here goes nothing.* She stuck the clip in the key-shaped hole and wiggled it. It bumped against something, then something else, then seemed to catch. She held it firmly and twisted. There was a click and the door's latch gave way. *It worked. Joan's idea worked.* Kiki felt a bead of sweat run along her cheekbone.

With trembling hands she pushed the door open enough to slip inside. *What if someone else is there, guarding Mama?* For a moment, terror gripped Kiki. Then Daddy's smile, the one he reserved for Mama, popped into her head. The last thing he'd said, months ago when he left for Germany? "It's up to you girls to take care of your mother while I'm gone."

She leaned against the door, felt it snap shut behind her. The small space, though lit only by twilight, felt bathed in sunshine compared to the stairway. Kiki stumbled forward as her eyes adjusted.

The room's iron cot stood against the wall across from the door. The two adjoining walls—an old wardrobe on one, a tiny table and chair on the other—were shadowed, but visible.

"Mama?" The form curled up on the cot, one bare leg and foot hanging down, didn't move. Kiki leaned in, breathing the familiar, flowery scent of her mother's sweat-dampened hair. "Mama?" Mrs. Moore's black eyelashes fluttered open. "Kiki?" A sob came from her bruised and bloody mouth.

Kiki knelt by the bed. "I'm here, Mama. See? It's me. Your Kiki."

Mrs. Moore nodded. Her eyes closed.

"You want me to untie you?" *Dumb question. Of course, she does.* Kiki pushed back the chenille bathrobe draped over her mother and cringed. Mrs. Moore's arms were twisted behind her, the wrists bloody beneath stringy, scratchy-looking twine. One ankle was tied to the cot.

"They hurt you!" Kiki saw a long, hand-shaped bruise on her mother's cheek. *Daddy will make someone pay for this.* She swiped at the tears suddenly in her eyes and whispered, "We'll get them for this, Mama." The corner of Mrs. Moore's mouth twitched in what might have been a smile.

I have to signal Harold. I have to get Mama untied. Kiki felt panicked. *How bad is she hurt? What if she dies? What if Harold goes home and doesn't come back?* She forced herself to breathe.

"Too bad we don't keep knives up here, huh, Mama?" Kiki looked around the room. Other than the furniture, it was bare. No dishes, no silverware. Just the empty table, the wardrobe ... She stepped over to the tall, freestanding closet and opened the double doors, willing them not to squeak.

It was empty of everything, even coat hangers. Kiki frowned, closed the doors and pulled open the drawer below. It was empty, too. As she pushed it closed something sparkled, just for a second, in a crack along the bottom. *What's that?* She looked closer, digging at it with her two unbitten fingernails. A point emerged: a metal point. *It's a nail file. Holy cow.*

It was stuck very deeply in the drawer's bottom edge; it had been in there a long time—maybe since before Kiki was born. *How do I get it out?*

She glanced at her mother and froze. Hovering above Mama's bruised cheek was a familiar, transparent form: the little boy ghost. As Kiki watched, horrified, he ran a finger along the bruise on Mama's cheek. Almost silently the words, '*Wo bist mutter?*' Where is my mother? touched Kiki's ear.

Mama made no response. *Did she hear him? Does she know*

he's here? Kiki sat back on her heels. *Doesn't look like it. What should I do? It's a fine time for him to show up! Will he tell Gisela and the man I'm up here? No. Has he hurt anyone, so far? No. I'll pretend he's not here.*

Kiki tiptoed to the window, avoiding eye contact with the ghost child. She studied the rolled-down blinds. *How do I keep them from rattling when they roll up?* Instead of pulling on the center cord, she held the blind's bottom corners and tugged, guiding the stiff cloth as the inner spring recoiled. The blind rolled soundlessly up. *Yes!*

She glanced at the ghost. Still hovering near Mama, he clapped his hands—they made no sound, of course—and smiled. *What do you know? You're just a little kid. Or were.* Kiki's mouth twitched in a smile of her own.

She turned to the uncovered window and looked out, trembling slightly at this new level of exposure. In the yard below, half-hidden by rhododendrons and white birch trees, Harold and Roland stared up at her.

Relieved sweat broke out on Kiki's forehead. She waved, then dropped her hand to her side. *How do I signal that I found Mama and he should go for help?* She waved her arms, pointing toward the street and mouthing, "Go for help!" Harold shook his head at first and then nodded, turning toward the street and disappearing from view. Roland backed into the bushes and disappeared.

Kiki pulled the shade down and knelt next to Mama. "They're going for help. You'll feel better when I get you untied." Her anxious whispers got no response. Kiki sat back. *Is Mama asleep?* "Don't be dead, Mama. Please don't be dead."

"*Die muter ist verletzt.*" The ghost appeared again, hovering next to the cot and looking up at Kiki.

"*Verletzt?* Hurt? Oh, you mean she's not dead?" Kiki felt a rush of relief. "*Danke sehn,*" she whispered. *I guess he should know.*

She stepped over to the wardrobe, knelt next to the open drawer and pulled at the file with the tips of her fingers: nothing. The file refused to budge.

Darn it all! Let's see: maybe I could use the hairpin again. She couldn't help smiling as the mass of growing-out frizz came loose a second time. *That awful perm is good for something, after all.*

The end of the hairpin worked even faster than in the door lock. The file loosened almost immediately. Kiki eased it out, inch by inch, until the flat, rough metal fell against the palm of her hand.

Swallowing a screech of delight, she scurried across the floor to her mother, applying the file to Mrs. Moore's bound wrists. The twine, bloody now and with bits of skin stuck to it, broke apart quickly. As it fell away, Mama moaned softly.

"Sorry, Mama." Kiki's lips moved in a silent prayer. *Please take over here, God. This is way more than I can handle.*

Sawing through the twine around Mrs. Moore's ankle took only a minute. When the file broke through and jerked upward in her hands, Kiki whispered, "There! You're free, Mama."

Mrs. Moore made a futile effort to sit up. One hand came up, blood running down the wrist, to touch her daughter's cheek. "My baby," she whispered.

"I'm not a baby!" The automatic response—this was a standing joke in the Moore household—brought a tiny smile to Mama's face.

CHAPTER TWENTY-THREE

Mama's eyelashes fluttered open. She looked into her younger daughter's anxious face. "Where's Joan? They attacked me. For no reason." The words, though slurred, were indignant, unbelieving.

"I know, Mama. They're bad people. Joan's at Peggy's house. Do you think you can climb down a tree?"

Mama's eyes closed again. She shook her head.

Kiki looked around the room. *We have to get out of here, but how? Mama can't even stay awake.* Her gaze went past the little ghost, now curled up next to Mama like a wispy, contented puppy. *Too bad we can't go through walls like he does.* She shivered. *That would mean we're dead.* She ran her hands through her frizzy hair. The impossibility of the situation— Mama hurt, *Nazis* downstairs, a ghost acting like the family pet —was overwhelming. Kiki got to her feet and tiptoed to the window, pushing between the blinds for a patchwork view of snow, tree tops, and the house next door.

Why is there light coming from those windows? Daddy said no one lives there. As she stared through the darkness, headlights appeared at the entrance to the next-door driveway. An Army Jeep rolled in and stopped at the front of the house. Two men—*officers in uniforms just like Daddy's*—climbed out and stood for a second, looking around.

If this window opened, I could scream for help. Maybe I can break it. No. I'd just cut myself. Look up here, officers. Up here! Kiki waved frantically as the men went up the steps and inside, not looking her way even once.

"Kiki?" Mama's voice, so weak. "Get out of here. Don't let them catch you." Her eyelids twitched, trying to open. "*Dumbkopf herr* ... hit my head ... hurt me." She sank back against the mattress.

Leave you, when I finally found you? I don't think so. Kiki knelt next to her mother. "Don't worry about me, Mama. I'll figure something out." She glanced at the wispy outline of a child tucked in next to Mama. *Does Gisela know this house is haunted? If she's afraid of ghosts, maybe he could help us.*

The tiny spirit yawned, opened his eyes and stuck his tongue out. As Kiki watched, fascinated, he rose into the air and began buzzing around the room. His expression—eyebrows and mouth turned down menacingly—matched the ominous grey color of his small shroud.

"You want to scare someone?" Kiki tried not to smile. "Go downstairs. Go chase away those Germans, *mach nicht!*"

The ghost didn't seem to hear her. He zoomed to the window, smashing his face against the glass and squealing, **OOEEE!**

"For crying out loud, watch where you're going!" Kiki's attention went from the little spirit who, unhurt, was backing off for another collision with the window pane, to the scene beyond the window. Something was moving, something low to the ground and stealthy. It crept toward the back of the house next door.

Is that Roland? Why didn't he go with Harold? What is he up to?

As Kiki moved toward the window a woman's high-pitched, *"Du bist eine swinehund!"* came from the yard below. This was followed immediately by a deep, growling, *"Dumbkopf! Saugling infant!* Moron! Suckling baby!*"* There was a low "Oof ." Then, silence.

Kiki stepped away from the window, thoughts of Roland forgotten. *Gisela and the man. They're right below us! Did they see me?*

An instinct to hide made her drop to the floor. She looked across the room to her semi-conscious mother. *I can't panic. I have to stay calm. For Mama.* She whispered, "Let's see: They don't know I'm up here. I have to keep it that way." *It's okay I'm talking to myself if it helps me stay calm.* She frowned at the ghost—*I hope no one can hear me*—and tiptoed back to the window.

They were arguing. Someone got slapped. The yard was cloaked in darkness. Kiki could barely make out, against the night sky, the shapes of trees, foliage, and the shed. *There's something on the ground, something lumpy. A person? It's not moving. Maybe they dropped a coat.* The sound of the slap echoed in her brain. *Where'd they go? To the shed? Back in the house?* That thought chilled her. "Please God," she whispered, "keep them away from us."

Her attention went to the trees where, a minute ago, she'd seen what might have been Roland. *It couldn't have been him. He went with Harold. Didn't he?*

WOOF! WOOF! WOOF!

Deep, furious barking broke the evening quiet.

*It **is** Roland! Where is he? Why is he barking? Darn it! I can't see a thing!*

Suddenly, lights went on next door. A man shouted above the barking. "Roland? For Christ's sake! Who let you out?" A deep, very familiar voice.

Daddy? Kiki gasped. *It can't be him. He's away on maneuvers.*

An impulse to scream, to pound on the window for her father's attention, died when Kiki heard, "*Gott in Himmel! Das hund! Wo ist er?*" in the yard below. She ducked out of sight.

WOOF! WOOF! WOOF! Roland didn't sound quite so frantic now, but he was still barking. Kiki heard Daddy say, "Okay, big fella, simmer down. Sergeant Wayne, at ease while I take my dog home."

As Kiki watched, half afraid she was dreaming, Colonel Moore and Roland came around the back of the house next door and strode into the darkness along the driveway. *Daddy's coming here! Hooray!*

Kiki tiptoed across to the cot and knelt next to her mother. "Mama, guess what? I just saw Daddy! He's not on maneuvers like we thought. He's doing something else for the Army. And he's next door! He's coming to our house right now." She stopped talking. Her mother was asleep, or ... *Not dead. I see her breathing. Maybe she's unconscious.* Kiki stood and hurried back to the window. *I have to get Daddy's attention, but I can't leave Mama. What should I do?*

Kiki heard the back door open and close, then the front door. *That's odd. Is Daddy here already? He wouldn't just hand Roland off and leave, would he? Roland wouldn't go for that.* She tiptoed over and put her ear to the door. Daddy's deep, slightly raspy voice floated up, garbled: "Looking for my wife ... the girls AWOL ... new *fraulein*, too ... Let me know soon as ..." *Is he on the phone? Why isn't he talking to Gisela?*

WOOF! WOOF! Roland began barking, loud. Through it, Kiki heard her father's "Halt!" Then the entire downstairs was quiet. *Did he leave? With Roland?* Kiki strained her ears to catch any sounds.

Click! *That's the front door. He's gone!* Kiki ran from the attic room, panicked. She was half-way down the stairs when she heard, "Kiki! Don't leave me!" Mama, weak and desperate. Kiki turned around and went slowly back up the stairs and into the attic.

"I'm still here, Mama. We missed Daddy." She gulped back tears. *What do I do now?* She rushed to the window, pressing her cheek against the pane. From the yard below she heard an odd sound, like someone clearing his throat. Then, *"Was ist los?"* – angry, whispered words uttered directly below the window.

As if he could read her thoughts, the little ghost appeared at her shoulder. He stepped through the window pane, rolled himself into a ball and shot out of sight. A second later Kiki heard her father's, "What in the Hell?" and Roland's nervous "Grrr." Kiki smiled. Colonel Moore shared her ability to see ghosts, but he considered it a curse and wouldn't talk about it.

Now, flashes of light bobbing in and out of the bushes showed two dark shapes moving furtively. *Is Daddy coming back?* The light went out. Seconds later the figures of a man and a dog appeared in the open yard.

Can they see me? No. It's too dark. God, please don't let them run into Gisela and the bad man!

Daddy's boots crunched on the snowy ground. Kiki heard him whistling softly, "O Tannenbaum," as he strode toward the back of the house.

The crunching stopped. The flashlight went on. Kiki saw her father and Roland kneeling next to the bundle of cloth. "What in the hell?" Colonel Moore sounded worried.

It's just an old coat, Daddy. From her vantage point Kiki could see a corner of the shed. It didn't look quite right. *That last bush could be a person. Watch out, Daddy!*

Without thinking she pulled off her boot, stuck her fist in it and punched the window pane. The glass, thick, hand-poured old stuff, responded with a **'Thump!'** A crack appeared and traveled out from the point of impact, but the pane didn't break.

Roland looked up, ears cocked, but Colonel Moore didn't lift his head..

I'll try again. Kiki had her arm raised when she heard her father's gruff, *"Halt! Wer gent dahin?"* Who goes there?

Beyond the circle of Colonel Moore's flashlight Kiki saw a shadow pull away from the shed. It lunged at Daddy. His hand went up; there was a loud **CRACK!** and the flashlight fell to the ground.

The yard, the street, seemingly the whole world stood still for a split second. Then from next door someone shouted, "Colonel Moore, was that you? Grab your weapon, sergeant! Shots fired!" Feet pounded on the driveway.

"Was that ... gunshot?" came whispered from the cot.

Kiki croaked out, "I don't know, Mama. Maybe." She stared out the window, willing her eyes to see in the dark.

Something moved halfway between the shed and the corner of the house. Moved and whined. *Roland.* He hovered over something, wagging his tail.

"Okay boy. I'm okay. *Halt. Offenzee.*" Daddy's voice, strained.

Daddy's alive!

The flashlight came on again. Kiki watched as her father got slowly to his feet, his sidearm hanging loosely from his hand.

"Daddy!" As she raised her hand to pound on the window. a high-pitched squeal came from the pile of clothing.

"Ach du Lieber gott! Du hast ihn vernichten! You killed him!" Colonel Moore's light shone on Gisela, sitting up now and crying.

"Ja vol, Ich ...." Daddy muttered hoarsely.

"Colonel Moore, sir?" Worried calls came from the Moore's front yard.

"Back here. Shot an intruder on my property."

Kiki's legs felt wobbly. She dropped to the floor, feeling for Mama's hand. Wordlessly, she buried her face in her mother's shoulder.

"S'okay, honey. S'okay." Mama's murmur was sweet.

Lights and loud, masculine voices drifted up from the yard below. Shouts of,

"What the Hell?" and "Holy shit, Colonel!" mingled with Roland's excited barking. Kiki heard her father say, "The *herr* is a stranger but that *fraulien*—she was in the kitchen with Mrs. Moore this morning."

For a long moment Kiki blocked out the turbulence beyond the window; it felt so good, just holding onto Mama. When Mrs. Moore whispered, "Do they know ... we're here?" Kiki groaned. "No." She sat wearily up. "I'll be right back."

"Don't leave me, honey." Mama's whisper was faint.

Kiki shuddered. *How can I tell Daddy where we are without leaving the attic?* She took a last look out the window: Two extra-big Jeeps pulled into the yard, making deep tracks on the sodden lawn. MPs—Kiki knew them by the red and white armbands—climbed out and hurried over to Daddy and the man on the ground. When an MP ushered Gisela gently to the front of a Jeep, a tiny voice squeaked in Kiki's ear. *"Sie entkommt!"* She's getting away!

Kiki looked over her shoulder at the little ghost hovering there. "Why do you care? She can't hurt us anymore. And she certainly can't hurt you. Wait a second: Is she part of the group that, er, 'took' your mother?"

The little ghost buzzed in a circle around Kiki's head, moaning, *Mama, mama. Wo bist mama?*

"I wish I knew, little guy." *I wish I knew your name.*

CHAPTER TWENTY-FOUR

Kiki looked down into the yard, where the man her father shot lay on a stretcher. Colonel Moore stood near the street, talking to someone in a Jeep. Kiki looked, looked again. Light glinted off red hair in the Jeep's passenger seat. *Harold?*

Suddenly Daddy straightened, turned and ran back into the yard. Harold jumped from the Jeep and loped after him.

Where are they going? Tell Daddy we're up here, Harold! A s she turned away, light brushed against the window's cracked pane.

"Anybody up there?" Daddy's voice, tense and gravelly.

Kiki felt a whisper of movement; cold fingers brushed the back of her neck. She turned to see Mama, on her feet and leaning toward the window.

"That you, Emily? My God!" The light went out. Daddy called, "Lieutenant Samuels? Over here. On the double!"

The front door slammed, so hard the house shook. Roland's

high-pitched bark, from somewhere inside, almost drowned out the sound of feet thumping on the stairs. With a splintering crash the attic door flew open. Kiki, one arm around Mama's waist to keep her upright, threw the other arm up to protect their faces. *J ust in case.*

Daddy, Roland, Harold and an M.P. burst in and skidded to a stop. "Emily? Kiki?" Daddy's words sounded tentative, as if he doubted what he saw. Then, as Harold and the M.P. stared, he gathered his wife in his arms.

Kiki moved away from them, feeling awkward and unimportant. While Daddy and the MP gently but persistently got Mama to tell them what had happened, Kiki leaned against the wall and closed her eyes. *It's over. Mama's safe now.* Exhaustion hit; Kiki felt dizzy. She slid slowly down the wall and closed her eyes.

"You were right. You were so right. Let me be the first to say, 'Good job, kid!'"

It took Kiki a second to realize someone was whispering in her ear. She opened one eye. There was Harold, so close she could feel the warmth of his breath. He had dark circles under his eyes and his freckled cheeks were pale, but he managed a smile.

"Thanks for coming back." Kiki returned the smile. Roland, next to Harold, whimpered. "You, too, boy." She nuzzled the dog's furry neck.

"You didn't think ...." Harold's whisper was interrupted by an MP saying, "Uh, Colonel Moore, sir? Should we call the medics?"

"Damn right. On the double. And I want both of those Germans detained."

Colonel Moore spoke into a walkie-talkie, then turned his

commanding officer gaze on his daughter. "Front and center, kid. What the hell happened here?"

Kiki got wearily to her feet, grateful that Harold did the same. Both stood at attention. "Yes, sir?" Kiki whispered.

The little ghost chose that moment to reappear, hovering by Kiki's shoulder. Kiki didn't see him; she felt a chill, though, and was about to turn her head when she saw her father's face reflect confusion, then somber acceptance. *It's the ghost, and Daddy sees it.*

"This whole mess is about the shed; am I right, Squirt?" Daddy's voice had lost its authoritative tone. He sounded very, very tired.

"Yes, sir." Kiki, Harold and the ghost all nodded. Kiki raised her hand. "Permission to speak, sir?"

Colonel Moore suppressed a smile. "Permission granted."

"Those Germans—our *frauliens* and that mean *herr*—they're looking for something on our property. That's why they hit Mama and stuck her up here." Kiki gulped. "That *herr* you shot? He's the one who grabbed me."

"Is that true, Emily?" Colonel Moore's voice had the most serious tone Kiki had ever heard.

Mama nodded, reaching for Kiki's hand. "Our girl found me, Bill. She even figured out a way to cut me loose." She held up her scratched, bloody wrists.

Colonel Moore looked away, shaking his head. He turned and, **Wham!** slammed his fist into the wall. Kiki and Harold both cringed. The ghost swooped up to the ceiling and disappeared.

"You want to know what they're after, sir?" Kiki croaked.

Colonel Moore shook his sore hand and nodded. She continued, "The people who lived here before the war? Mrs. Brown found out they were rich. And they had a little boy."

"Get to the point, Squirt." Colonel Moore's voice was hoarse. "The medics'll be here any minute."

At that moment the ghost reappeared, buzzing around Kiki's head and chanting, "*Nazis! Nazis! Nazis!*" She ignored it. "The people who lived here before us hid their gold and their child in the cellar. I found it—the gold. And a little skeleton."

Colonel Moore's eyes widened. "A child? That accounts for the ..." he glanced at the ghost, then at Harold. The teen was listening intently to the conversation. The Colonel cleared his throat. "You're telling me you found the former owners' treasure? It's still here?" He sat back on his heels. "We knew homes were still being targeted for looting—that's what these maneuvers were about." He put his hand over his eyes, squeezing away tears. "Dear God. They tortured my wife while I was not thirty yards away."

A siren wailed outside, then abruptly stopped.

"Medic's here." Colonel Moore looked out the window. "Their best man is on duty tonight, Emily." He went to the top of the stairs, balancing anxiously on the balls of his feet, then looked back at his wife. 'I'll follow you in the Jeep after I see to those *dumbkopfs.*"

"Can I go with Mama?" Kiki knelt timidly by the cot.

Colonel Moore shook his head. "The corpsmen don't need a kid underfoot." He turned away—the medics were coming up the stairs—and then looked back. "You did good today, Squirt. Stand down now." He reached out and tousled Kiki's hair.

Harold, Roland and Kiki were the last to leave the attic. At the threshold Kiki stopped, looking back into the small, dark room where she'd found her mother. *Is it safe to leave?* Every instinct screamed, *No!* Sweat trickled down her forehead. "Harold?" Her whisper seemed lost in the noise-filled stairway.

Harold didn't turn around. Roland, though, looked back at her and began barking.

The stretcher had reached the second-floor landing. The corpsmen glanced back and Colonel Moore tossed a, "Roland! Quiet!" over his shoulder before hurrying on. When Roland began whining, Harold looked back. "You okay, Kiki?"

She managed to shake her head.

"Something's wrong with Kiki, Colonel Moore." Harold's voice cracked. "I'll give her a hand."

"Much appreciated, young man." Daddy glanced back up the staircase. His face, what Kiki could see of it in shadows, was closed, sad.

Harold took the steps two at a time, stopping one step down from Kiki. "What's up?"

"I—I don't think I can leave." Kiki's teeth chattered; she felt like she couldn't breathe.

Harold reached out awkwardly and put an arm around her.. "Yes, you can." He looked anxiously into her eyes. "One step at a time. I bet you're in shock. I learned about that in Scouts." He eased her down from the top step, then the next.

At the second-story landing Kiki panicked again, clutching his jacket and whispering. "N-no. I can't."

"Close your eyes." Harold sounded nervous. "I'll guide you. C'mon."

She did as she was told. Immediately she felt Roland's fur —he was at her side—and something damp and foggy against her cheek. *The ghost? You're with me, too? Who are you, anyway?*

A high-pitched, lisping voice murmured, *Gustav. Mama calls me Gus-Gus.*

Kiki took one step, then another. *Gustav. What a lovely name.* She concentrated on the feel of Harold's warm, slightly scratchy hand in hers and took another step.

"We're at the second-floor landing now. Reach out. Grip the stair railing. Step down. That's it. You're doing great."

With her eyes closed Kiki felt, as well as heard, a cacophony from the front yard—the stinging cold of the outside air, the slam of the ambulance doors and the revving of a motor. She stopped, hoping to hear little Gustav's voice through it all. *Where did he go? I hope he knows I haven't abandoned him.*

"You made it! See?" Harold crowed.

Kiki opened her eyes. It felt strange being on the ground in the side yard after so many hours of watching from the third-floor window. With the spotlights and clusters of activity--- Daddy and an MP standing over the German man, another MP talking into a walkie-talkie, officers with clipboards making notes—she was overwhelmed by the frenetic, circus-like energy. "They took Mama already?"

"Looks that way." Harold, suddenly awkward, dropped her hand and waved to a Jeep pulling up in front of the house. As Kiki watched, the vehicle's doors opened and Joan, then Peggy and Mrs. Brown climbed out. Joan spotted her and hurried across the yard.

"Kiki! Where's Mama? Is she okay?" Joan achieved a personal best for shrill, almost shrieking tones.

Mrs. Brown and Peggy nodded to Harold and, without a word, wrapped Kiki in a hug.

Kiki took a breath and relaxed. *It's really over. Mama and I both survived.* From around Mrs. Brown's shoulder she said, "Mama went to the hospital, Joan. She's hurt, but Daddy said she'll be okay."

"Daddy? He's here?" Joan looked across the yard, saw her father and stopped. "What going on? Isn't he supposed to be on maneuvers?"

"I'll find out. You children stay right here. That's an order." Mrs. Brown strode across the mushy grass to Colonel Moore.

"So, Kiki?" Joan hissed. "What kind of hornet's nest did you stir up this time?" She leaned in near Peggy. "When we lived in Napa, she found a dead body and almost got herself killed."

"Really, Kiki?" Peggy turned away from Joan, her face shining with admiration. "What an exciting life you lead!"

"Yeah," Harold chimed in. "You should be grateful, Joan. If it wasn't for Kiki your mom would've died."

"Joan? Kiki?" Colonel Moore came across the yard with Mrs. Brown. "You'll be guests of the Browns tonight." His tone softened. "I'll pick you up in the morning. I imagine you'll want to see your mother."

Joan's face crumpled. "Is it true, Daddy? Mama's hurt?"

"Go on, now." Daddy's voice broke. "Your mother's going to be just fine." He straightened his shoulders, giving Mrs. Brown a quick salute. "*Danke sehrn.*" Thank you.

As Mrs. Browns' Jeep pulled away from the curb, Kiki looked back at the third-story window. It was dark, but she thought she saw something move. *The curtains? No.* Something pale and small separated from the window and swooped up into the darkness. *It's Gustav. Poor thing. He's still stuck there.*

"Oh, by the way, Kiki," Mrs. Brown's voice was soft. "I found some information about your house. The child who lived there with his mother and grandparents? His name was the same as my dad: Gustav."

Kiki sat up, startled. "Do you know where Gustav's mother is now?"

"The notes didn't say. Most likely the family escaped. Or were captured." Mrs. Brown's voice trailed off.

Harold straightened. "If you have their name, Mom, we could look for them on that memorial in the cemetery."

"I think it was Grossberg. Yes. I'm sure. The two G's, Gustav and Grossberg." Mrs. Brown smiled at Kiki in the rearview mirror.

CHAPTER TWENTY-FIVE

The next morning found Kiki and Harold at the gates of the lonely cemetery.

"Over there, remember? This front part is for Catholics." Harold pointed to the flat, untended back section, where the original stones lay helter-skelter on the ground.

"That's right. Beyond that ugly statue and through the fence." Kiki walked as fast as she could, her boots sinking into the snow. At the entrance to the Jewish section she dropped to her knees. "Here it is. Help me clear the snow."

Minutes later she sat back, clasping her sopping wet mittens and staring at columns of names carved in marble.

"Horrible lettering. Like out of the Dark Ages." Harold ran his finger down one column and up the next. "Let's see: Is this a G?"

Kiki leaned over his shoulder. "Maybe. Yes. Ga—here's the Ge's—Gr—oh, no!" She sat back, feeling suddenly weak.

"What?" Harold's hand went to the column where she'd stopped. "Oh. *Jah.*" Without looking at Kiki he read, "Grossberg, Jacob, Anna, Joanna." It's them. Your house's owners."

Kiki got slowly to her feet. "I have to tell—" she stopped. *Harold doesn't know about the ghost.* "Uh, never mind. I need to tell my dad we found them." She turned and trudged away through the snow.

"Hey, wait up. We're leaving already? We just got here." Harold sounded irritated.

Kiki stopped, suddenly very tired. "I don't like cemeteries after all, especially this one. The names on that plaque? They're all people who shouldn't be dead." She stamped her boot in the snow. "I hate this place!"

"Yeah. Me too." Harold's shoulders drooped. He looked desolate. "Let's get out of here."

When they reached the Browns' house, Kiki she sat down on the bottom step. "It's going to be weird going back to our house." She stared at her hands.

"Yeah, creepy weird." Harold blew out a breath. "Maybe your dad'll get you different quarters."

Kiki sighed. "Not likely. He doesn't believe in special treatment." She got to her feet. "I am going to ask if the little skeleton can be buried next to that memorial, though. That's not special treatment. That's just right."

Harold pushed off from the porch railing and started up the steps. "Maybe my mom can throw her weight around and get you guys a different house. I mean, she is the General's wife. Hey, Mom!" He opened the front door and went inside.

Kiki flopped onto her stomach and watched as an ant pulled a bit of leaf through the snow. She thought of little Gustav, alone in the house on *Vierstrasse. I have to tell him I've found his mom.*

"Come on in, Kiki. I made sandwiches." Peggy appeared in

the doorway.

"Can I eat out here? I'm waiting for my dad." Kiki sat up and hugged her knees. .

Peggy sat down on the step. "Are you okay, *cherie*? You've been through more the last twenty-four hours than most people in a lifetime."

Kiki looked up, startled at being called *cherie*. She'd forgotten the Browns' last posting was in Louisiana. "Yeah, I'm okay."

Both girls were silent. Then quietly, tentatively, Peggy said, "You went to the cemetery? You're so brave." She chuckled. "Joan worries about you. Did you know that? You keep running around, saving people—she's afraid one of these days she'll lose you."

Kiki looked up, startled. "Are you kidding? Joan hates me. She tells people I'm retarded. To her, I'm an embarrassment."

Peggy shook her head. "That's just her cover; she doesn't like being compared to you because she thinks she doesn't measure up."

The ant and its' trophy-leaf were gone, probably in a gap between the snow and the soggy ground. Kiki turned a puzzled face to Peggy. "I seriously doubt that. She hates that I'm ... sensitive." *Maybe Peggy isn't like Joan. Maybe she's nice.*

Kiki took a breath and let it out slowly. "We went to the cemetery to look for the Grossbergs."

"On that memorial?" She looked at Kiki. "Were they there? That charm you found, the Menorah. They were definitely Jewish." She ran a hand across her face.

Kiki nodded. "*Jah.* I'm going to ask my dad to have the skeleton put next to that memorial."

Peggy looked surprised. "You'd do that? Tell you what: I'll mention it to my mom. That way, it will get done for sure." She hurried up the steps and inside.

Kiki was half-way up the steps to follow Peggy inside when

she heard the growl of a motor. Colonel Moore's Jeep rounded the corner and pulled to a stop in the driveway.

Daddy hopped out and ran around to the other side of the Jeep, opening the side door as he called, "Give me a hand with your mother, Squirt."

Mama's back!

"You bet!" Kiki pushed off from the steps, yelling, "Joan! They're here. Both of them!"

After a tearful reunion in the Browns' kitchen, Mrs. Brown clucking over Mama like a mother hen and the teen-agers eating a mountain-sized stack of sandwiches, Daddy rapped his knuckles on the table.

"It's time for the Moores to head out. We need to reclaim our home. I went by earlier; there's an M.P. posted at the shed but the house is cleared for occupation." He turned his drill-sergeant gaze to Joan. "Your mother will be off her feet for at least a week. You—with Kiki assisting—will be in charge." He glanced quickly at Mama. "We'll get a new housekeeper, but it may take a while. Your mother will be hand-picking this one."

Joan's eyes slid toward Kiki; she straightened her shoulders. "Yes, sir," she chirped.

Kiki palmed her badly-bitten fingernails and raised her hand.

"Speak up. This isn't school." Daddy sounded almost indulgent.

"Yes, sir. I mean, No, sir. I just wanted to say I'll do my best to be a good assistant to Joan. We'll take really good care of Mama and the house."

A few minutes later, as the Moores helped Mama into the Jeep, Colonel Moore put an arm around Kiki. "I've had those remains moved from the shed, Squirt. They'll be interred near that Memorial in the Bad Kissengen cemetery."

Kiki's mouth fell open. Before she could speak he continued, "If we went through proper channels it'd take months, maybe years. We have to live in that house, though, so the place needs to be cleaned out now—the skeleton, the treasure, *everything*." He raised his thick black eyebrows. *"Verstehen?"* Understand?

Kiki threw her arms around Daddy's waist and whispered, " *Verstehen*, Daddy. I'll make sure little Gustav knows where to find his mother."

ABOUT THE AUTHOR

B. Payton Settles writes what she knows; all of her stories are set in areas where she has lived. She comes from a family of writers—her paternal grandparents ran Kansas newspapers—and a highlight of both high school and college was the editing of the schools' yearbooks. She lives in California, enjoying retirement from a career as a Reading Specialist.